P9-EME-535

Jocelyne Saucier
translated by Rhonda Mullins

Coach House Books, Toronto

First English edition, second printing. Originally published in French in 2011 as *Il pleuvait des oiseaux* by Les Éditions XYZ inc.

We acknowledge the financial support of the Government of Canada through the National Translation Program for Book Publishing for our translation activities. Published with the generous assistance of the Canada Council for the Arts and the Ontario Arts Council. Coach House Books also appreciates the support of the Government of Canada through the Canada Book Fund.

LIBRARY AND ARCHIVES CANADA CATALOGUING IN PUBLICATION

Saucier, Jocelyne, 1948-
And the birds rained down / written by Jocelyne Saucier ; translated by Rhonda Mullins.

Translation of: Il pleuvait des oiseaux.
Issued also in electronic format.
ISBN 978-1-55245-268-4

I. Mullins, Rhonda, 1966- II. Title.

PS8587.A386331413 2012 C843'.54 C2012-905221-3

This title is available as an ebook: ISBN 978 1 77056 333 9.

Purchase of the print version of this book entitles you to a free digital copy. To claim your ebook of this title, please email sales@chbooks.com with proof of purchase or visit chbooks.com/digital. (Coach House Books reserves the right to terminate the free digital download offer at any time.)

for Marie-Ange Saucier

In which people go missing, a death pact adds spice to life, and the lure of the forest and of love makes life worth living. The story seems far-fetched, but there are witnesses, so its truth cannot be doubted. To doubt it would be to deprive us of an improbable other world that offers refuge to special beings.

This is a story of three old men who chose to disappear into the forest. It's the story of three souls in love with freedom.

'Freedom is being able to choose your life.'

'And your death.'

That's what Tom and Charlie would tell their visitor. Between them they have lived almost two centuries. Tom is eighty-six years old and Charlie is three years more. They believe they have years left in them yet.

The third man can no longer speak. He has just died. Dead and buried, *Charlie would tell the visitor, who would refuse to believe him, so long had been the road to reach Boychuck, Ted or Ed or Edward – the variations in the man's first name and the tenuousness of his destiny will haunt the entire tale.*

The visitor is a photographer who is as yet unnamed.

And love? Well, we'll have to wait for love.

THE PHOTOGRAPHER

I had already driven many kilometres of road under threatening skies, wondering whether I would find a clearing in the forest before nightfall, or at least before the storm hit. I had travelled all afternoon along spongy roads that led to labyrinths of quad trails and skidding roads, and then nothing more but clay ponds, beds of peat moss and walls of spruce, black fortresses growing ever thicker. The forest was going to close in around me without me laying my hands on Ted or Ed or Edward Boychuck, whose first name changed but whose last name remained the same, a sign that there was some truth in what I had heard about him, one of the last survivors of the Great Fires.

I had set out with directions that seemed sufficient. *At the end of the road that runs along the river, turn right and keep going for about fifteen kilometres to Perfection Lake, which is easy to spot with its jade green waters – glacier water from the Quaternary Period – and shaped like a plate, perfectly round, that's where it gets its name, and after looking out over the jade plate, take a left at the rusted-out mine headframe, keep going straight about ten kilometres, be sure not to take any of the crossroads or you'll end up on the old logging roads, and then, you can't miss it, there is only the one road leading nowhere. If you look to the right, you'll see a stream that cascades into volcanic rock – that's where Boychuck has his cabin, but I might as well tell you, he doesn't like visitors.*

The river, the jade lake, the old headframe. I had followed all the directions, but there was no cascading stream or cabin in sight, and I had come to the end of the road. Farther along there was a fallow field, barely in good enough shape for a quad and not something my pickup would want to cross. I was wondering whether I should backtrack or settle in for the night in the back of the truck when I saw smoke appear at the base of a hill and form a thin ribbon swaying gently above the trees. It was an invitation.

Charlie's eyes, once they spotted me in the clearing surrounding his collection of cabins, gave off a warning. You don't set foot on his property without an invitation.

His dog had announced me well before my arrival, and Charlie was waiting, standing in front of what must have been his living quarters, since that was where the smoke was rising from. He had an armful of small logs, a sign that he was about to make his supper. He held the load against his chest throughout our exchange, which kept us outside a door he clearly had no intention of opening to me. It was a screen door. The other door, the main one, was open inward to let the heat of the blaze escape. I couldn't make out anything inside the cabin. It was dark and chaotic, but the smell it gave off was familiar. It was the smell of woodsmen who have lived alone, steeping, in the forest for years. Mostly it was the smell of unwashed bodies; I had never seen a shower or a bath in any of the living quarters of my old forest friends. It was the smell of burnt fat; they mainly ate fried meat, thick stews and game that required a good dose of grease. The smell of dust fossilized in layers on anything that lay still. And the stale smell of tobacco, their drug of choice. Anti-tobacco campaigns hadn't yet reached these men. Some still chewed their square of nicotine and religiously snuffed their Copenhagen. It's hard to understand how much tobacco meant to them.

Charlie's cigarette roamed from one end of his mouth to the other like a small tame animal, and when it finished burning, it rested at the corner. He still hadn't said a word.

At first I thought it was him, Ed Boychuck, or Ted or Edward, the man who had survived the Great Fires and who had fled from his life into the forest. He was spotted only occasionally at the hotel where I had spent the previous night. The hotel was preposterous, a huge construction in the middle of nowhere, with three storeys of what had probably been the height of elegance, now a relic of civilization lost in the woods. The man I took to be the owner but who was merely the manager – *Call me Steve,* he said after we exchanged a few words – told me that the hotel was built by an eccentric with cash to burn, a Lebanese man who had made a fortune in doctored liquor and had then set about losing it in megalomaniacal construction projects. He believed that the railway would make its way toward what promised to be a new Klondike, and he wanted to be the first to snatch up the business that was sure to follow. His final obsession, Steve said. The new Klondike was nothing but a big hoax, and no train appeared spewing its steam in front of the Lebanese man's luxury hotel. He went to the States, where he expanded into a chain of hotels for truckers.

I like places that have given up any pretence of stylishness, any affectation, and that cling to an idea waiting for time to prove them right: prosperity, the railroad, old friends ... I'm not sure what they're waiting for. The region has a number of these sorts of places that stand the test of time as they revel in their own dilapidated solitude.

My host at the hotel had talked all evening about the hardships of the place, but I wasn't fooled. He was proud to tell me stories of bears devoured by ticks and the hunger that waits outside your door, of the moaning and creaking carried on the wind at night, and the mosquitoes, *don't get me started on the mosquitoes, they all come out in June, mosquitoes, black flies, no-see-ums, deer flies, it's better not to wash – there's nothing like a thick hide to protect you against the little beasts – and the cold of January, good god!* The cold of January. There is no greater source of pride in the North, and my host wasn't going to let the chance slip by to complain about it so that I could quietly admire his courage.

'And Boychuck?'

'Boychuck is an open wound.'

This silent, motionless man on the doorstep couldn't be the man I was looking for. Too calm, too sturdy, almost debonair in spite of his eyes searching mine for what they were hiding from him. *Animal* was the word that sprung to mind. He had the gaze of an animal. Nothing fierce or threatening. Charlie was not a wild animal. He was simply on the lookout, like an animal, always asking himself what lay behind a movement, a flash of light, an overly emphatic smile, or words that sounded too smooth. And my words, in spite of the conviction I put into them, had not yet persuaded him to open his door.

You don't just land on the doorstep of someone who has lived close to a century with an improvised spiel. You need tact and skill, but not too much. Old men know a thing or two about the art of conversation. It's all they have left in their final years, and words that are too slick make them wary.

I had started with a few words about the dog, a lovely animal, a mix of Newfoundland and Labrador, who had stopped barking but was keeping an eye on me. 'Nice dog,' I said, as much to praise the dog as its master. 'Labrador?' The only response I got was a nod of the head and a look that said he was waiting for the rest. I hadn't come all this way to talk about his dog.

'I'm a photographer,' I told him straight away. I had to dispel any misunderstanding. I wasn't selling anything, had no bad news to deliver, wasn't a social worker or a nurse, and most certainly wasn't from the government, the worst of the lot, as I had learned from all the elderly folks I had visited. *You're not from the government, I hope?* If I took too long to explain my presence, the question was never long in coming. *We don't want some bureaucrat coming here telling us something's not quite right about our lives or about our papers, that there are letters or numbers that don't add up, that something in the files is suffering from inconsistency. And what about me? You don't think I'm suffering? Vamoose, government, go on, scram!*

'I'm a photographer,' I repeated. 'I take pictures of people who survived the Great Fires.'

Boychuck lost his whole family in the Great Fire of 1916, a tragedy he trailed behind him wherever he tried to make a life.

The man I saw before me carried no such wound inside. He was smooth and compact, a monk in stone. He seemed impervious to everything, until I saw him lift his eyes to the sky, grow sombre at the threatening clouds, which were growing heavier, more laden – Charlie's eyes, when they returned to me, held the lightning of the coming storm. An animal, I thought again. He responds only to nature.

I explained what had brought me there, taking care to give him names: I had met so-and-so who told me about someone who knew someone else, I explained the trail I had followed, all the old acquaintances who, each in turn, served as safe conduct and led me here. 'A very nice spot, I can see why you choose to live here, Mr. Boychuck, with this magnificent lake at your feet and all this beautiful nature surrounding you, but if you have a moment to spare, I'd like to sit down with you and talk about all this.'

It was dishonest. I knew I wasn't talking to Boychuck, but a bit of wiliness is sometimes necessary.

Boychuck's name affected him more than he would have cared to show. I saw his eyes falter, and then the sky darkened, the earth grew flatter, the storm raged with impatience, and Charlie's voice was finally heard.

'Boychuck is dead and buried.'

He was not going to tell me anything more. I felt in his manner that the interview was over and that I should go back to wherever I had come from with the little I had just learned. He was about to turn his broad rustic back on me when the skies opened up. It was coming down as if from a showerhead. With a movement I barely felt, a gesture of natural authority, he opened the screen door and, his hand on my back, heavy and light at the same time, pushed me inside.

'Get inside. You're going to get wet.'

The voice was no more amiable than the rest of him. He went straight to his stove, a miniature wood stove – I had never seen one so tiny – and stoked his fire without giving me a second thought. The fire was dying. He had to restack the kindling, blow on the blackened embers, add some bark, blow again, and when the flames leapt to life, he closed the stove door and vents and went to what, in the darkness, I took to be his kitchen counter. Judging from the number of potatoes he was peeling, I took it that I was invited to stay for supper.

The rain on the roof was deafening. It was falling more heavily, and at times we could no longer hear each other, and then the wind chimed in, gusting, surging and howling, and the thunder and lightning came. We both knew I couldn't go back to my pickup.

'You'll have to sleep here.'

I impressed him more than once during the evening. About a fern, lichen or shrub I knew the name of, while he, who had intimate knowledge of them, couldn't name them. He could describe a plant from the underbrush with the precision of a master botanist – its companions, its habits, how it collects the dew, protects itself against dryness and windburn – all without knowing its name. 'It's wild lily-of-the-valley,' I told him, after he wondered whether the plant's fruit was truly venomous. Partridge poison, that was his name for it, a lily of the underbrush. 'The fruit is edible,' I explained, 'but in moderation. If you eat too much, it can give you the runs.'

'How do you know all that?'

I am not a botanist, a naturalist, or anything like that, but twenty years of wandering in the company of such folks gave me a certain familiarity with the forest. I had made it something of a speciality. I used to call myself a vegetative photographer, because of all the veins of leaves I stooped over to capture on film and the contemplative life I led. At some point I got tired of it. I wanted to return to humanity. I wanted faces, hands and eyes; I could no longer lie for hours in wait for a spider to trap its prey. Chance put me on the trail of the Great Fires, or their survivors, all very old folks of course because the first Great Fire was in 1911, and that's where the conversation ground to a halt. Charlie refused to go on once the subject was broached.

But the evening was pleasant nonetheless. He was delighted for the company, you could tell. His features relaxed, but you couldn't hear it; he still had that grumbling, resonant voice that had made such an impression on me when I arrived.

We talked about our lives, mine on the road, searching for a new face or a new encounter, and his in his cabin, watching time go by, with no worry other than living. Even that was a lot, according to him, and I had no trouble believing him, because there is plenty to do to avoid freezing or starving to death when you're living alone deep in the woods. I emphasized the word *alone,* but he smelled the trap. He was a trapper, so he had an instinct for danger, and he wasn't going to let himself be caught in such a poorly laid device.

'I have Chummy,' he said, indicating the dog with his eyes.

The dog was sleeping fitfully near the door, each clap of thunder making his fur bristle head to tail until the flat calm returned, when he slept, his breath deep and regular, until the next crash.

As soon as the dog heard Charlie speak his name, he got up and went to lie at his master's feet.

'Eh, Chummy, tell our guest how we make a good team, you and me.'

Charlie's hand meandered through the dog's fur, stopping at the neck and at the base of the ears, where it detected clumps that it removed in small woolly tufts. It roamed, soft and vigorous, an expert at scratching and massaging, along the length of the dog's body. Chummy grunted contentedly while his master continued his conversation with the visitor, every once in a while tossing a few words his way.

'Isn't that right, Chummy, aren't we good together?'

I was impressed by the thick, coarse hand, stiffened with age, that became pliant and supple in his dog's fur, and even more so by the voice that, when it spoke to the dog, softened, becoming velvety and intimate. He explained in this tender bass voice that Chummy was afraid of storms. 'It's the thunder that scares him,' he said. 'You have to reassure him, so that's why I keep him inside when there's a storm.' The cello voice trailed off somewhere, and he resumed that tone of the lord of the forest who won't let himself be imposed upon.

The supple hand and velvety intimacy of the voice came back a little later when he unrolled the bundles of fur to make my bed.

The storm had not waned any. The roof dripped smack in the middle of the one-room cabin. Charlie knew the leak and had placed a pot on the floor. The *tink* of the water in the pot, the rain drumming on the windows, the crackling of the fire in the stove, and Chummy snoring comfortably under his master's stroking: the cabin was filled with the sounds of a warm, comfortable life. I was delighted to have been invited to stay.

I slept in a bed of furs like a princess in a fairy tale. A soft layer of black bear, silver fox, ash grey wolf and even wolverine, a deep brown that glistened with a flash of jet black on my bed of pelts. Charlie was impressed that I could identify them, particularly the wolverine, which is a rare animal, even rarer in hide form, because it is reputed to be aggressive and intelligent and hard to trap. 'But with the price we get for pelts,' he said, 'trapping isn't worth it anymore.'

The bundles of fur were piled in a corner. There were at least twenty of them. 'Very practical during the bitter cold of the winter,' Charlie said in answer to my astonished eyes, and I imagined him at minus fifty, buried under a mountain of pelts, Chummy probably in bed with him, and the cabin silent other than the stove burning a blazing fire.

He had stopped trapping since environmentalists had caused the prices to plummet, but he kept his last catches, and with each pelt he unrolled, the story of the animal that had left him its skin came to him. His voice slowed and became rounder as the animal came back to mind: where it lived, the trail it took, how the animal came to be caught in the trap, all this he told me in a warm, enveloping voice. 'Poor little mother,' he said, caressing a beaver pelt with the leather of his hand. 'She shouldn't have been there.'

I like stories. I like being told the tale of a life from its beginnings, the twists and turns and the sudden jolts way back in time that make it so that a person finds himself sixty years later, eighty years later, with that certain gaze, those hands, that way of telling you that life has been good or bad. An old woman, among all the ones my search led me to, had shown me her hands, two long hands, fine and white, that rested on the floral pattern of a dress and then spread out on the table. 'Look,' she told me, 'not a mark, no wrinkles. They are just as they were when I was twenty.' Her hands were the trophy she was proudest of. They told of five children born one after the other, a farm that went up in smoke, a husband who disappeared in the Great Fire of 1916, a cramped dwelling in town, hungry children, and household after household after household that paid wages, an entire life spent in soapy water and not one flaw. Not one crack.

'Poor little mother,' Charlie said, and I felt like we were in one of those great stories about life that I love so much. The beaver, a four-year-old female, was caught in Charlie's trap with three barely formed little ones in her belly. 'She shouldn't have been there. It was the male I was after, the large gingery male, almost blond, a rare colour, a valuable fur. I knew the whole family that lived in a lodge on a narrow bay of the lake. There was the mother who was preparing her nest for the spring, three young from the previous spring's litter, and the big golden chief who refused to be caught in any of my traps. I got one of the young males in January and then another in February, nice catches, but nothing like the gilt of my chief. Normally, I close my traps in March. Fur loses its lustre as springtime approaches, but I was reaching, I wanted gold, and I left my traps open. Poor little mother. She should never have come out of her lodge.'

There was also the story of a fox cub that caught its paw in a hare snare and cried like a baby, of a wolf that had followed him and watched him all along his trap line, of a spring bear he stumbled upon. It took me a while to get to sleep amid all the lives he had told me about. It was as if I could hear the wolf, the fox and the mother beaver sigh nostalgically at the telling of the lives that had been theirs and that I was using as bedding. The smell of animal was strong and heavy. I tossed and turned, searching for a breath of air that wasn't filled with their odour. And then there was Charlie's snoring, which at times reached deafening heights and trumpeted a fanfare along with the roar of the thunder.

I woke up late. The cabin was warm and still. The only sound was the crackling of the fire in the stove. Just as I was dropping back to sleep, I felt Charlie's eyes upon me.

He was sitting at the table in a halo of grey light. A beam of silvery dust bisected the room from two tiny windows facing each other. At the centre of the beam of light was Charlie's white head haloed in grey like a religious icon. He looked at me attentively, perplexed, a look full of questions.

I usually sleep naked and for a moment I thought I had taken off my clothes in my sleep. A quick look reassured me. I still had on my jeans and my sweatshirt, but I understood what intrigued and worried the old man, because I found myself in an unfortunate position, my nose buried in a mass of black, woolly fur, my arm draped over a warm body, and my hand in the curve of the animal's belly. I had slept with Chummy.

We quickly hauled ourselves out of bed, Chummy and I, to join Charlie, who had not said a word about this state of affairs. Instead he started reassuring me about the day ahead, a way of saying that good weather had returned and letting me know that I no longer had any reason to hang about these parts.

But he invited me to stay for breakfast. The menu featured more potatoes, this time fried with diced bacon, and very sweet tea.

The conversation would not get off the ground; there was some kind of uneasiness. Charlie answered my questions with grunts. I am not easily defeated, but this time I had to accept that I was going to leave without getting anything out of Charlie, not even another trapping story. And then the miracle occurred.

The door opened and Tom walked in.

'Sorry, I didn't realize you had a fiancée.'

You could tell straight off where Tom came from. He didn't need to tell his story. His voice, burnt by drink and cigarettes, attested to years spent hanging around in seedy joints. Large, bony, a few hairs scattered over a bald head, one eye steady and the other wandering – exactly the opposite of Charlie.

His good eye scanned the room, and when he found what he was looking for, a metal bucket that he overturned to make a seat, I realized I was sitting in his place.

'What brings you to this neck of the woods, my lovely?'

I'm not the type of woman men spontaneously chat up. I have a build that commands respect and a stare that transforms the overly solicitous into a pillar of salt, but I was delighted with 'my lovely,' salacious chivalry from an old man who wanted to get across that he knew his way around women, and I leapt at it to bring me back to my quest, the Great Fires, Boychuck supposedly dead and buried, but who might still be found in perfect health somewhere in a cabin if I let the old man's swaggering run away with him.

Tom had known neither the Great Fires nor the Boychuck who had roamed for days through the smoking rubble. 'Who do you take me for, Methuselah?' he said, planting his good eye on mine. 'I'm too young to know about things that happened before Noah. I'm the youngest one here.' In spite of his pretensions to youth, he told me the old tales I already knew, the woman who gave birth in the lake where the town had sought refuge, the other woman who had thrown herself into the wall of flames and the child who followed, and the woman of whom all that was found was a wedding band among the ashes. He told me about all this intertwined with his own stories, with no concern whether or not I believed them, as if to say, *if you don't believe me, it's because you haven't lived.*

From what he told me, I understood that he had been a gold smuggler, a dangerous occupation, if you can call it an occupation, similar to the young people of today who cross borders with cocaine hidden in their suitcases or their intestines. Tom regularly made the trip by train to Toronto and New York with gold nuggets tucked inside his guitar because he was also a musician, true or false I'll never know, just like the rest. There was a bit of everything that morning at Charlie's table. There were love stories. A woman cried out his name on a station platform, the train started moving, the woman was still crying out, a Russian princess who danced the flamenco at the hotel where he was performing and who held a little baby in the air while the train carried Tom away. And then, suddenly, his life became the life of the lame: he took a serious beating when he tried to go behind the back of the high grader who had hired him. He waited for the miners at the site office and had started to trade nuggets with them for himself when his employer's goons arrived.

'Don't believe me? How do you think I lost my eye?'

And while he continued – because his life didn't end with his infirmity, he had his legs broken, his ribs bashed in and one eye destroyed, but his heart was intact, he had other loves, other adventures – and while he told me about this incredible life, I asked myself who this man really was. He wasn't the sort to cling to the solitude of a cabin in the middle of the forest.

Charlie was watching me with an amused smile. He had been listening to Tom's stories for a long time, the truth and the lies, and no doubt wondered where I found myself in the mixed bag of tales.

They made an odd pair. Charlie, a big grumpy bear who had a hard time hiding the pleasure he took in the conversation, and tall raw-boned Tom, who was trying to hold my attention by any means.

What was this crank doing in the forest? Men who spend their lives steeping in grimy hotels normally grow old there. I have met broken-down old men, barely able to raise their glass, who live like shadows among the beer drinkers and feel right at home there. They have their table in a far corner, and from time to time someone will buy them a drink, other drinkers who feel like having an old man at their table. People ask them for their story, tease them, ride them a little and then forget about them. They retire at their regular time for a nap in their room, normally in the basement, a dark, damp room, often windowless, stinking of old socks and tobacco. They wouldn't know what to answer if asked if they are happy. Happiness is beside the point. They have their freedom and fear only the social worker who could come take it away from them. That's exactly what Tom answered when I asked him what brought him to the middle of nowhere.

'Freedom, sweetheart, the freedom to choose how you live.'

'And how you die,' Charlie added.

And they roared with laughter.

Tom had lived in one of those cavernous hotels. He swept up, washed glasses and chased flies. He had been given the title of caretaker, but that fooled no one. It was a way of sparing the pride of an honourable drinker who had seen better days. Tom had knocked back more than his share, mainly of scotch. *Scotch was my drink. I can still hear the ice tinkling in the glass. Just thinking about it gives me the shivers.* He was able to forget his age and get hammered like a young man. His binges lasted days and nights and ended in delirium and vomit. Which one day led to a coma, the hospital and a social worker. *A woman even huskier than you, if I may say so.* The rather ample social worker grew attached to the old man and that was the end of poor Tom's freedom. The even-huskier lady wanted him to be happy in a tidy little room at a seniors' home, and she waged a fierce battle to have his physical and mental decay, his alcohol-induced senility and his legal incapacity to manage his own affairs recognized. She even tracked down his two children, a greying man and woman who vaguely remembered having seen him during their childhood, to sign the papers.

'I was ready for the trash heap!'

'When he got here,' Charlie said, taking up the tale, 'he looked like a hare who had just outrun a pack of wolves.'

I didn't find out how he made it to this hideaway in the middle of the woods, except that the decision was swift and final.

'In two minutes, I had packed my bags and was on the road to freedom!'

And again he burst out laughing, accompanied by Charlie, who had abandoned any reserve and was letting go a throaty, booming laugh. The two old men were giggling like kids at the idea of this blow against all the social workers of the world who wanted to lock up old men in old folks' homes.

Charlie had forgotten that he was mad at me for having slept with his dog, and his eyes were almost smiling when they looked at me. He got up to put water on to boil, and while he rummaged in his pots and pans, Tom launched into a volley of digs and diversions as if he were back in one of the hotels where he had made a career as a drunken clown, and I alone was playing a room full of people laughing.

'You see that old guy playing the housewife? Well, he's not really there. He's a ghost. He's been dead for fifteen years. What did you call it again, Charlie?'

'Kidney failure.'

'Kidney failure, that's what the doctor told him, and three sessions of what? To die slowly but surely?'

'Hemodialysis, three sessions of hemodialysis a week.'

'That was three too many, and Charlie here tipped his hat to all the nice folks who wanted to help him, and that's how come he's here today making us tea. I don't suppose you have any sugar cookies, do you, Charlie?'

They would have gone on that way, and between the two of them I would have heard Charlie's story had I not seemed so interested in the conversation. Tom's eye narrowed to the point of becoming a black slit, while the other, the wandering one, went off in every direction to finally light upon me.

'You're not from the government, I hope?'

I asked myself which of the two was alive, Tom's eyes I mean, if the marble eye was the good one or whether I should follow the one that was wandering. This man had more than one trick up his sleeve. He was capable of great tomfoolery, but make no mistake, behind the clowning was a cunning old fox, and the wandering eye could very well have been the one that ransacked your insides while the steady eye held your attention.

'Because if you're government, I might as well tell you right now, you'll find nothing here. As far as anybody's concerned, we don't exist anymore.'

The time had come to tip my hand – my bag – and to show them the photos in my portfolio, otherwise I was going to lose the trust I had earned. I normally save this moment for the end of the meeting, when I sense that I have to leave a mark for the next one. The photo session takes place at the second visit. The subject has had time to sift through memories and secretly wants me to come back. Nobody can resist the idea of being the centre of somebody else's attention. The most stubborn old man turns as smooth as honey when he sees me coming the second time. I arrive with my gear. My tripod, my Wista with bellows and my dark cloth. I take photos the old-fashioned way, for the precision of the grain that seeks out the light in the creases of the flesh and for its ceremonial slowness.

My portfolio has around a hundred pictures, portraits for the most part, but also snapshots taken off the cuff with my Nikon, the sole purpose of which is to tame the subject at our first meeting.

Charlie recognized no one in my photos, but Tom spotted a few acquaintances. A woman with eyes a delicate shade of blue, Mary Gyokery, whom he had met on a friend's arm. Peter Langford, a tall rack of skin and bones who had been a champion boxer. Andrew Ross, his eyes veiled with cataracts, a toothless smile, who kept me for a full day in his small two-and-a-half telling me about the four hours he spent in Porcupine Lake while the town burned. Samuel Dufaux, the miracle survivor, who was discovered in a stream splashing about with a dog that had been placed in his care. His mother had run to the house to help her husband fight the fire. Dead, both of them. Tom had known Dufaux as an adult, rich and partying. He had just discovered a copper vein and was celebrating at the hotel where Tom played guitar. He had pockets stuffed with money and plenty of friends around, and he woke up the next morning with nothing left. No money, but happy. He could go back to sampling rock in the woods.

'And Boychuck? Was he a prospector too?'

I already knew that Boychuck had sampled rock for a time, but the opportunity was too good to pass up.

Tom's eyes almost came together.

'Ted is dead, sweetheart, just last week. I still have the blisters on my hands from digging his grave.'

Blisters on his hands, give me a break. These old guys had palms that were callused to the bone. A few hours of shovelling wasn't going to do them any harm.

I couldn't help a little smile. That's what convinced them, my sceptical smile, to take me to where they had buried Boychuck. To satisfy my curiosity and then, adios visitor, I would have to go back to where I came from. Nothing was said, but it was understood.

So we left in a procession, Tom, Charlie, me and their two dogs, because Tom had his as well, a golden lab by the name of Drink, in memory of the tinkle of ice.

We walked along the shore of the lake for about a hundred metres, and then we headed back into the forest on a well-cut trail, machete marks still fresh and the ground almost smooth. It was like walking on carpet.

A dog came to meet us. It was a strange one, a less-than-successful mix of malamute and Labrador, but most of all it was the animal's eyes that weren't quite right, one steel blue and the other velvet brown. I felt like I was being watched by a third eye planted in the centre of the malamute's arabesque forehead.

'Kino, Ted's dog,' Tom said by way of introduction.

At the end of the trail, the dogs ran to a cabin surrounded, like Charlie's, with a collection of constructions. It was an enchanting spot. The hill that sloped gently to the lake was covered with a potent green, a forest of conifers that absorbed the light of the beautiful sunny morning and scattered it like a long tranquil river. The calm was majestic. The island of shacks, nestled in a large clearing of forest at the foot of the hill, had something movingly fragile about it: a small observation post with its back to the ramparts of the forest, with the great expanse of lake laid before it. I imagined Boychuck's mornings spent contemplating all this.

What they pointed out to me as his grave could well have been just that. The earth had been recently disturbed in an area that could have accommodated a man of average height, but there was nothing to indicate that anyone had been buried there. No cross, no inscription, nothing that could have testified to the presence of someone buried below and, what made me doubt Boychuck's body was there, a complete lack of reverence on the part of the two old men. They lit a cigarette and talked quietly between themselves. They raised no objection when the dogs took turns lying along the rectangle of funereal earth.

It was time to go. There was no longer any reason to linger. Nevertheless, I asked how he died.

'He just reached his expiration date,' Tom answered. 'At our age, that's how you die.'

There were no goodbyes. They let me leave with no other send-off than a wave of the hand when I turned toward them before taking the trail back to my pickup. Chummy, the only civilized one in the bunch, accompanied me as far as the trail. I had time to take a few pictures before Charlie called him back.

On the way back, I tried to imagine the thoughts running through poor Charlie's mind. I had called out to him that I would bring him the pictures of his dog. He thought he was rid of me, and now he had to contemplate a next time.

I got lost on the way back. My landlord's directions from two days prior were no longer as clear, and I got confused in a tangle of paths that led me to a lake bathed in light, the same lake that welcomed my aged friends each morning, along the shore of which ran a road in compact, solid sand that led me in a straight line back to the forsaken hotel.

My innkeeper had made a mistake. He had made me drive a long loop of needless kilometres to the west when there was this road to the east that led directly to Boychuck and his companions.

They had a protector, a man who fielded questions from travellers, spouting nonsense, sending them on wild goose chases. He was the gatekeeper of their hideaway. I was both intrigued and moved by such precautions to protect a free, hardscrabble life in the middle of the forest.

Boychuck or no Boychuck, I knew I would be back.

The story has another witness, and he is about to arrive on the scene.

To look at him, you would put him in his early thirties, but he is over forty and is only twenty in his mind. He has long, lithe muscles, hair in a ponytail at the nape of his neck, a hoop in his ear, and if one were to go further, say, inside his head, one would find it brimming with ideas; he is always on a quest for something.

He drives a Honda TRX 350, a recent model, and tows a mini trailer along the road that runs beside the lake. When he arrives within sight of Charlie's cabin, he raises his eyes toward the roof, a gesture he always makes, to check whether the chimney is smoking, whether Charlie is there, alive.

He is a regular visitor to this place.

He comes less often in winter. He arrives with his big snowmobile, a Skandic, a powerful machine that's not afraid of deep snow and that he sometimes drives full throttle over the frozen lake. Standing on his thoroughbred, he surfs the dunes of wind-hardened snow, flying from dune to dune, testing the void, the feeling of leaving it all behind, of soaring above himself. He gets drunk on the speed and the cold, and then heads back toward Charlie's cabin. He can see the three columns of smoke rise up into the sky.

He is also a free man, but he is not the gatekeeper.

His name is Bruno.

BRUNO

They took no pride in telling me that they had had a visitor. She claimed to be a photographer. But first they had to tell me that Ted had died. I should have expected it. He was so old. Too old to make the effort to die, it had seemed to me.

Just reached his expiration date, Tom assured me, and I sought out Charlie with my eyes. The two of them formed a sound box. When you wanted to know whether Tom was telling the truth, you looked at Charlie. There wasn't a note of dissonance in Charlie's eyes. Ted had indeed died of natural causes.

The three of us knew why that was important to know.

The three old men had a death pact. I won't say suicide, because they didn't like the word. Too heavy, too sad for something that, when all is said and done, didn't intimidate them that much. What was important to them was being free, both in life and in death, and they had come to an agreement. There again, no oath with hand over heart, no sorrow, just each other's word that nothing would prevent what had to be done if one of them fell ill to the point of no longer being able to walk, if one of them became a burden to himself or the others. The agreement didn't apply for a broken wrist or arm – a one-armed man can still get by, but the legs, there is nothing more important in the forest. Locomotion, as Tom would say, emphasizing the O's as if by uttering them they would get up and walk. The agreement also said that if necessary, they would help. They wouldn't let their friends fade away in suffering, left without dignity, staring up at the sky.

I had been told about this a long time ago. By chance of conversation: they weren't the sort to make bell-ringing revelations. When something important happened, they muttered it just like anything else – Charlie in particular, who was a world-class mumbler. As for Tom, he'd never lost his hotel hustler's patter, and he turned everything into a joke. But you couldn't go by that; his hawk eye was lying in wait for you. He was the one you had to talk to. As for Ted, you had to pay close attention to follow his ruminations.

Conversation always took place in Charlie's cabin, which was the most comfortable. Tom's was a dump. We would spend hours there, sometimes entire days, playing cards while letting our thoughts reveal themselves.

Ted didn't join us, never did, but I know he was bound by the agreement.

'Our death is our business,' Tom had said.

It was February, a snowy, blustery day, one of those days that keeps you inside near a roaring fire, and we were in the middle of a poker game. I had arrived two days earlier. In winter, I came less often. I would arrive a bit like Santa with my sack of supplies. My snowmobile sled was full: fruits, vegetables, fresh, moist cakes for the old guys, and more substantial treats, like parkas, long underwear, a chain saw, a gas lantern, sometimes newspapers too. It amused them to see how the world was getting on without them.

This time, I had a gas auger. A major innovation, as they would no longer have to break their backs using their ice pick. The auger would make a hole in the lake in no time, and they would have as much water as they needed. And fish, added Charlie, who had wanted to try the tool on a neighbouring lake where the pike, he claimed, were so black they were blue. But a blizzard blew in and kept us playing poker for two days, although Charlie wouldn't let it go; he wanted his midnight-blue pike.

'Tomorrow, whether it's snowing or blowing or shit is falling from the sky, I'm going fishing,' he announced, along with his full house.

'And who's the one who's going to find you, all frozen and contorted?'

Tom's hand wasn't very good. He had a pair of jacks.

'Don't worry. I'm going to make sure I have a smile on my face when I go.'

My hand was no great shakes either. Not a single pair and this stupid question.

'You still want to face death head on, Charlie?'

Silence and knowing smiles from either end of the table.

'So neither of you is afraid of dying?'

I was an idiot, really.

'Go get your salt box, Charlie.'

The box was on a shelf above Charlie's bed. A small tinplate box holding white crystals the size of pickling salt. Strychnine. Fox poison, they explained. Left over from the trapping days. It kills a fox in three seconds and a man in less than ten.

Each man had his own box of salt, and if one day he were called upon to help, each man knew where the other's box was.

I thought I was a tough guy, able to roll with the punches, but to hear them talk about their own deaths as if they were akin to taking a leak or crushing a bug, I felt sick to my stomach.

'Our death is our own business,' Tom said, as loudly as his scratchy voice would allow.

And then, more calmly, because he could sense my discomfort: 'You're too young. You wouldn't understand.'

Charlie, as was his way, let Tom finish his rant before adding his two cents.

'I've already had a second life free of charge. I don't see why I would have a third.'

I knew Charlie's story – he had told it to me. It wasn't your everyday story. Married, two children, a job at the post office, a weekend trapper. The trapper part really tells the whole tale. Trapping is more than an occupation, more than a hobby: something incongruous, an anachronism, an abomination – the thought of it, killing wild animals! The neighbourhood children would follow him down the road and spy on him through the small window in the basement where he scraped his skins. He could feel the terror in the whispers that reached his ears.

And yet it was in the forest that he was able to take his own measure as a man, breathe the air of the world, feel he was part of the power of the universe.

As he grew older, he had come to hope that he would die there one day, like an animal, no wailing or weeping, nothing but the silence of the forest greeting its creatures on their way to join the souls of the beaver, the weasel, the mink, the fox and the lynx, his true companions.

And then his doctor, in telling him about the kidney failure and three hemodialysis sessions each week, unwittingly offered him an honourable way out.

He was retired at the time; his children were long gone, and his wife had a pension. He put his affairs in order with the bank and the notary, and he headed off to await death.

'I moved into my trapping camp and I waited for death, but she didn't come. I got to thinking that I had been given a second life. I decided I would live this one on my own terms.'

He waited one more week and then he left his camp as if he were off to his trap line.

'I'm pretty sure they searched for my body, but my trapping ground was so big. They could have assumed anything: that I had drowned myself, that I was rotting somewhere in the muskeg. Pronouncing me dead wasn't a problem, I'm sure of that.'

And kidney failure?

'I piss as good as the next guy. Doctors aren't magicians. They make mistakes just like anyone. Mine got it wrong.'

So Charlie had arrived one day with his pack, and Ted let him move in near his camp. Tom arrived a few years later. Ted must have decided that they had what it takes; otherwise he would never have allowed it.

Ted was a broken soul, Charlie a nature lover and Tom had seen everything a man is allowed to see. The days passed, they grew older together and they reached a venerable age. They had left behind lives they had closed the door on. No desire to go back to them, no desire other than to get up in the morning with the feeling of having a day all to themselves and no one to find fault with that.

The three of them formed a buddy system that provided enough range and distance to allow each of them to believe he was alone in the world. Each one had a self-sufficient camp with a view of the lake, but they couldn't see their neighbours. They had taken care to leave a thick buffer of forest between them.

Charlie's camp was the best maintained. Four cabins: one for living, one for firewood, one outhouse and one for storage. Nothing was left lying around, no shovel, no axe. Nothing was neglected, while at Tom's cabin, you had to look at the chimney to guess which one was his living quarters, everything was so cluttered and battered.

As for Ted, no one had set foot in his cabin. It was impossible to trace the path of his thoughts on the walls, impossible to know what his eyes came to rest on. Ted hid himself away for days, even weeks during the winter months – and the winter months are interminable in the North. They would see his tracks in the snow, so they knew he had gone to collect the hares from his snares. They would see a nest of wood shavings near his wood storage shed, so they knew that he had stocked up on kindling. But they didn't see him, for months they wouldn't see him, and then suddenly he would appear.

I hesitate to say that Ted was a painter, so little did what we found in his cabins resemble anything at all, but that's what he did during the long winter months, and that's what convinced him to let me plant my pot in his forest.

I had arrived there on the trail of the Boychuck legend. The boy who had walked through smoking rubble, the man who had fled his ghosts into the forest, one of the last survivors of the Great Matheson Fire of 1916. I had heard the story here, there and everywhere. Small towns in the North collect stories. All you have to do is sit at a bar, and after two or three beers someone will sit down beside you and if you give them the time, they'll tell you everything you want to know.

An open wound, was what I heard most often.

That's what Steve told me too.

Steve is disillusionment personified, a man with no ambition or vanity. He reigns over his dominion with complete indifference. The hotel doesn't belong to him. The owner left it in his hands – abandoned it, really.

What I like about him is his faraway gaze.

We were on our second joint. Steve loves his pot. He inhales with a gusto I have never seen in anyone else.

We were settled into the languidness that I like, and he said, as if we had been discussing the subject for hours:

'It's the ideal place for what you're looking for.'

Neither of us had spoken about my plans for a plantation. But we both knew what we were talking about. I hadn't come to this part of the world to pluck petals off daisies.

'An ideal spot, but the old man won't be easy to convince.'

I left the next day down the sand road he pointed out, which led me directly to the old man's cabin.

Ted was waiting for me. He had heard me coming. This man knew his forest. He had heard the soft step of my running shoes on the sand, and he was waiting for me, sitting on a stump in front of his cabin, looking like someone lost in thought but aware of my presence. I could almost have heard my steps as they approached his ear had I not been deafened by the speech I wanted to give him.

Shaggy, tall and sturdy, in a plaid shirt and Big Bill pants, he was exactly what you think of when you think of a woodsman. He merely had to turn his eyes to me for me to understand that he had seen the world, and that he had had more than his share.

I was a young punk then, and he was already very old, so it was looking like the conversation would be difficult. He did nothing to help me. He let me get tangled up in a speech that rambled in every direction. I couldn't even understand parts of it myself. And he said not a word, made not a hint of movement on his stump. He let me dig myself deeper into impossible explanations until, no longer able to listen to myself, I decided to shut up.

He looked at me a while longer.

'It could be done,' he said, quite simply.

I had a moment of vanity believing that I had swept him up in the excitement, the lure of the illicit, the opportunity to thumb his nose at the world he had rejected. But I soon realized that the old man needed money. He negotiated the deal with the hand of a master.

He wanted linen canvas, sable brushes, hog's bristle, artist-quality oils, deep pigment colours. All this from Winsor & Newton, a reputable supplier, very expensive naturally, beyond his means, and found only in Toronto. He painted on plywood with frayed brushes and oils that didn't hold their colour. Steve took care of his supplies, but he went no further than the hardware store in the next town, two hundred kilometres there and back.

So Ted painted. It was hardly a mystery. His clothes were always stained when he came out of hibernation. The splashes of colour on his clothes never failed to surprise me. What he ordered from me were mainly dark colours. Coal black, ash black, smoke grey, an indefinable brown called burnt umber. But as to what was on his canvasses, none of us had any idea.

Ted's camp was midway between Tom's and Charlie's. Every morning after stoking the stove and a breakfast of potatoes with bacon, Tom headed off toward Charlie's cabin. Every morning, Tom passed by Ted's and glanced at his chimney. Whether it was smoking in a straight line, hiccupping little puffs or spreading smoke in a low cloud, it was all described to Charlie every morning in their first conversation of the day.

The smoke that rose out of Ted's chimney was the most reliable indication that he had gotten up that morning, lit his stove for his potatoes and bacon, resumed his thinking from the night before and started his day as a living, solitary man.

I studied the chimneys with the same attention. I had to expect that one day death would arrive before me. Strangely, I thought Tom would be the first to go. He was the youngest of the three, still full of the boisterousness of his former life, never settled, always telling stories about this and that, but battered by the follies of youth: blind in one eye, short of breath, a gimp leg. I never thought he had what it took, and yet he held his own.

They talked about death the same way they talked about the rain or nice weather. I would just have to get used to it.

'Nice day.'

'Yep. Nice day to die.'

It wasn't sad or painful, simply a possibility they raised like any other. They had a good laugh at having grown so old, forgotten by everyone, free agents. They felt as if they had erased their tracks.

As we sat in the cabin, Charlie and Tom were gently needling each other as always.

'Think you'll die today, Charlie?'

'If I have another night like last night, maybe tomorrow. But if it has to be tomorrow, I'd like it to be at sundown. I've always wanted to die watching the sun set.'

'So tomorrow at twilight.'

'Yep. At twilight. But if it's too long in coming, I think I'll wait. I don't want to die in the dark.'

'Not in the dark. If you're too picky, Charlie, she won't want you. You'll be over a hundred, and at that point, you're old, really old. You're worthless. You ain't even worth your shit.'

And Tom calling me to witness: 'This pighead will never make up his mind to die.'

And then silence. Which no one worried about. We were used to silence in which each one returned to his own thoughts.

This time, the silence was long, smoke-filled and heavy.

I knew the conversation wouldn't resume with something trite when Charlie hunched over his mug, threw me a look and went back to his cup, as if the news he were breaking were meant for the tea.

'Ted's dead.'

I should have expected it. It had to happen one day, but I wasn't ready. You never are, and it was a bolt of lightning. Something slicing straight through me.

Ted was a man made for eternity. He couldn't die in his bed like just anyone, with no other sign than a silent chimney.

All he had on was an undershirt and long underwear when they found him in his bed, half covered with a sheet, no sign of struggle against pain, and, Charlie hastened to add, no foam around his mouth.

'No foam? You're sure?'

I wanted reassurance. I never liked the idea of death by strychnine. They joked about it easily, but it wrenched my heart.

'Just reached his expiration date,' Tom said again.

And Charlie added that there was almost a smile on his face, so content did he look to be leaving.

'A smile for death is the final courtesy.'

Ted leaving a smile on his corpse. It was hard to imagine because I had never seen him smile.

I wanted to see where they had buried him.

So we set off. The dogs leading the way, Charlie's bear step heavy and silent, Tom limping along at his side and me bringing up the rear. You could almost have believed it was a nice summer day, that work awaited us somewhere and that Ted was sitting on a stump in front of his door expecting us. But Ted wasn't going to be joining us in our work any longer. No more felling trees for Ted, no more repairing the cabin, no maintaining trails, no more hunting moose. Ted was somewhere else, smiling down at his corpse.

Shoots of grass had started to appear on his grave, a rectangle of earth of very modest dimensions, it seemed to me, for the man he was. His cabin was a few metres away, lifeless, without the slightest wisp of smoke. It was toward the cabin that our thoughts went. The remains buried beneath our feet were nothing. Ted's true headstone was his cabin.

We had to go in. To pay our final respects or out of curiosity, I couldn't say. I was convinced that we had to go into his cabin, to see what his eyes saw all these years. Smell the odours that surrounded him. See, smell, hear, touch. We had to fill ourselves with Ted's life to say our goodbyes.

We went in. Me first, with Tom and Charlie hanging back for a moment. They had gone in to take out the body, but now they hesitated.

At first glance, it wasn't much different from Charlie's cabin. A twenty-square-metre room. Two windows facing each other. Under the right-hand one, a sink in old enamelled cast iron and a counter that was really just an extension of planks covered with linoleum, at the end of which the woodstove sat imposingly, the centrepiece of any self-respecting cabin. At the back, in the darkest corner, was the bedroom, a mattress on a wood base hewn with an axe. The dining room, unlike standard practice, was in the other dark corner of the room. A table, again in two-by-fours, and a single chair. Everyone knew Ted didn't entertain. And in the sunniest part, under the left-hand window, the one that was south facing, an easel, in the same two-by-fours, on which rested a canvas covered with a smoky grey streaked with black and a few dabs of colour. The colours were indistinct. Red, orangey or yellow, it was hard to tell. They overlapped, intermingled, consumed each other. It created the strange impression of a world dissolving in a muffled cry.

There were other canvasses propped up against the wall, covered with the same greyish coating and a few bursts of colour, like flutey notes in a requiem. Nothing terribly cheering. Nothing to leave a smile on a corpse.

We went through the other cabins.

Like at Charlie's lair, one was used for the woodpile, one was used for storage, between them was the outhouse, and in back, on much more careful foundations and completely closed up without a single window, a cabin with a lock on the door.

A lock in the woods. It was an insult. A serious offence. Ted knew it and still he had locked the door to his cabin.

We broke the lock with the butt of an axe, and we found ourselves in the presence of something unbelievable. From one end of the cabin to the other, canvasses similar to those we had just seen, hundreds and hundreds of canvasses, stacked one against the other, all creating the effect of being smothered while the world crumbles around you.

There was an empty space of a few feet amid the canvasses at the centre of the cabin, a sort of nave that received a bit of light from the door.

That's where we were, Tom, Charlie and me, asking ourselves what we were going to do with all this.

Tom thought we should let nature reclaim the cabin.

'Time will return all this to the earth.'

Charlie was not convinced.

'Ted didn't do all this to add a layer of compost to the earth.'

I wasn't sure of anything. My head was spinning. I suspected them of having waited for this moment to spring the other news on me.

'We had a visitor.'

They weren't proud of themselves.

Neither was I.

I too had a visitor to tell them about.

Now we have come to the third witness, Steve, disillusionment embodied, another man who has rejected the world. He found his freedom in managing a hotel that no longer serves any purpose. The only way to reach it is via a dirt road that intersects an isolated byway beyond which there is only forest and lignite, a poor man's coal that no one wants, and unless, like the photographer, you're drawn to the song of desolation, you'll feel that time has distended, that this place is out of sync with reality.

Steve is maybe fifty, maybe younger – he is ageless. He is the man who takes in the strays from the road.

What you have to understand about Steve and Bruno is that they are drawn to the illicit. Their friendship is based on their shared need to feel they are on the other side, on a slope that's a little steep, a little slippery, that they alone know about. It gives them an extraordinary sense of freedom.

Steve is tall, all arms and legs, with a tautness in his eyes and a special way of keeping the eyes of others at bay, but if your eyes hold his for a certain amount of time, he will lower his guard and let you approach. There is nothing he likes better than talking with strangers the road brings his way, even though he pretends otherwise.

Bruno is younger, more tractable; he has not renounced the world. He has friends everywhere. He comes and goes, is always on the move. He is the least pensive of anyone in this story.

They will have to put their flair for the illicit into action yet again, because another visitor is coming their way, and she will need a new identity and a new way to live her life.

STEVE

Her hair, above all her hair, that was what I saw first, a shock of white hair above the dashboard, hair so diaphanous it could have been light, a splash of white light, and under the radiance of the hair, two terrified black eyes. She was tiny, shrinking into the seat; I could see nothing else.

I had heard the motor of Bruno's Caravan and had gone outside well before he arrived. Seen from afar, the white spot on the windshield could have been anything. Bruno's van was loaded to bursting. Tools, building materials, clothes, special treats for the old guys.

It was only when he reached the level where I was standing that I understood that the white spot I had seen was the head of an old lady.

He greeted me as he always did, two fingers raised to his cap, which meant that everything was all right, but I could see from the slowness of his gestures that he was completely stressed out. Not a word, no explanation after the two fingers to the cap – all his attention was on the tiny little thing, the old woman, shrinking into the seat, whose large black eyes took in everything around her. She was delighted and terrified to be here.

Bruno gently opened the door, closed it soundlessly, and then with the tread of a wolf, with the tread of a cat, which was so unlike him, he went to open the passenger door, and the old woman slowly unfolded from the seat. Who was she?

I thought maybe a former wife. The old men had left behind full lives. I thought in particular of Charlie, who was duly married and could be reclaimed.

The old woman was truly tiny, the size of a twelve-year-old child, very fragile, a porcelain doll, and made only small movements. She leaned on the arm Bruno offered her, and with the tread of a teeny mouse, she let herself be led toward what I still called the Lebanese man's hotel in spite of the little of him that remained. The owner had not asked me to render accounts in years.

'The bags,' Bruno said, motioning to the back seat with his head, and I went to pick a brown suitcase off the heap, to the great relief of the old woman, who followed me with her eyes.

Slowly we arrived in the great hall, them in front and me behind. The room was intimidating, I admit. The few guests I had always circled it with their eyes suspiciously before entering. That's because hunting trophies that the owner and his friends had left behind were hung on the walls: moose antlers, gaping bears' mouths, lynx, wolves, clawed and hairy, with ferocious eyes, some stuffed in their entirety, arched on a pedestal, ready to pounce. The effect was striking. I had kept everything as it was, hadn't bothered to change a thing.

And here was this little old lady, who definitely bore no resemblance to an animal tamer, leaving the arm of her protector and creeping toward the most formidable piece in my bestiary, a wheat-blond lynx, growling with all the ferociousness its large pink muzzle would allow, immortalized in a powerful leap, its two front paws ready to rip in two anyone who approached. And that is just what the old woman did. She approached the pedestal, her gossamer head level with the back paws that anchored the animal's leap, and she remained there for a moment, still, not saying a word, and then she turned toward us. Her wrinkled face showed both fear and fascination with the fear. With a thin delicate finger, she pointed to the monster stuffed with blond fury. She had no idea what it was.

'It's a lynx, auntie, a lynx. Come sit down. I'll make you some tea.'

Auntie?

He sat her in a rocking chair near the window, her suitcase at her feet, and he went into the kitchen. I followed him. He had some explaining to do.

'Exactly what have you brought us?'

'I don't know what came over me.'

'Is she really your aunt?'

'My father's sister. I didn't even know she existed. No one knew.'

'Can you tell me why you brought her here?'

'I don't know why. You have to help me.'

He was nervous, lost in his gestures. He had decided to make her a sandwich and was looking for the ham in the cupboard, the bread under the sink. His hands came and went without knowing what they were touching.

'What's her name?'

'Gertrude.'

'You're not serious!'

'Yes, but we'll have to find something else for her.'

I only half understood, but I was reassured. If we had to produce fake ID for the woman, it wasn't hard. We had done it for Charlie, and then for Tom. I don't even remember their real names. Ted didn't need any, because he was running only from himself.

Bruno handled the paperwork, fake and real. He was in charge of external affairs. The old men and I took care of the plantation. It was an arrangement that had worked pretty well. In fifteen years, no one had come to sniff around in our plant beds. A few strays from the road, hunters and fishermen, sometimes came to get lost at my doorstep. They were looking for untouched spaces where man hadn't planted his astronaut foot. I sent them west. There were enough forest roads to keep them driving in circles for an entire afternoon. There were also nostalgics for the Great Fires, Ted's fan club: memoir writers, historians loaded down with tape recorders and cameras, and briefcases stuffed with papers. They stayed for hours talking about it and went home without further ado, happy not to have to get lost in the forest. They were satisfied with what I told them. The photographer was the only one I hadn't managed to scare off. A strapping woman, that one, even a bit husky. I would have to have a word with Bruno about her.

But for the time being, there was this little old lady waiting in the great hall.

'What's she done? Has she killed someone?'

'Right. With an axe and her little white hands.'

Okay. Serious conversation would have to wait.

We found her dozing in the rocking chair, her head hanging over her chest, arms resting on her thighs, hands open. She lit up the room. We backed out, which seemed to take an eternity, and slowly closed the door behind us, another eternity. The door creaked and whined because its hinges had never been oiled, and we looked at each other, astonished by our precautionary gestures, or embarrassed, rather. We weren't in the habit.

Now he had to explain what the woman was doing here. If it was just a matter of getting her fake ID, he didn't have to bring her to me. So whatever it was, it was a lot more complicated.

A lot more complicated, in fact, than anything I could have imagined. The story of Gertrude, who became, at our hands,

Marie-Desneige, was long. Very long. She was eighty-two years old when Bruno brought her to me, and her story had begun sixty-six years earlier when her father admitted her to a psychiatric hospital. She had been sixteen.

It was a horrendous story. I kept interrupting Bruno, because each new part of the tale added to the horror. I kept saying 'It's terrible,' him agreeing, 'Yes, terrible,' and he would continue, not happy about the story he was telling, but he would continue. We spent almost an hour getting indignant over Marie-Desneige's past.

Bruno didn't know why she had been committed. In fact, no one in Bruno's family had known anything about her. They didn't even know she existed. A letter was discovered after the death of Bruno's father, among the deceased's papers, in which Gertrude begged her brother to get her out of that hell. She was thirty-seven years old. The letter was dated May 15, 1951, and bore the letterhead of the Ontario Hospital, but the address, 999 Queen Street West, contained all the drama of a life – 999 Queen Street West was notorious throughout the province as the place in Toronto where thousands of the mentally ill were sent.

There was no further correspondence. No other trace of the woman who had signed *Your sister Gertrude* in the deceased's papers. The letter had gone unanswered.

'It's appalling, there's no other word for it,' is what I told Bruno, 'it's terrible,' and he nodded his head.

'Yes, it's terrible, and yet my father was a loving man. He raised us to care about others and to want to help, within reason. That's what defined my father, I think. Within reason. And it was the too-reasonable side of him that made him fear his sister's supposed insanity – "supposed" because she's not crazy, I'm telling you. She is in full possession of her faculties.'

'Sixty-six years in an asylum is not reasonable.'

'No, not exactly reasonable, but you have to understand.'

His father, his grandfather, his uncles, his aunts – all those who had come before him were guilty. A life had been wasted because of them. But Bruno couldn't help it. He had to defend his father and his blood.

'You have to understand. It was ignorance, the dark ages, the fear of anything that couldn't be seen or understood. It was the times.'

It wasn't like Bruno to defend the failings of another era. Nothing he was doing or saying was like him. He was nervous, agitated, his hands were fluttering like butterflies. His attention was elsewhere, behind him. He had his back to the window and couldn't see what I could readily see as I faced the window – it was fascinating, all the white spilling onto the old woman's chest, lighting up the room.

'Is she still sleeping?' he would ask occasionally.

'She's sleeping. Don't worry. Go on, continue.'

Because he had to continue, he had to explain why he had brought his elderly aunt to me, and what we were supposed to do with her. The problem wasn't in giving her a place to stay. I still had a few rooms that were presentable enough. The photographer had told me she had slept well here. No, the problem was more serious than that. I was waiting for the rest of the story.

The letter had gone unanswered. Bruno's father had to die for it to be discovered.

'My mother,' Bruno began, and I knew that it would get stuck in his throat. He had never had a good relationship with his mother.

'My mother couldn't bear it. The letter was written with impeccable grammar, not a single error of spelling or syntax. The handwriting was also remarkable: elegant, graceful, fine loops, downstrokes with pretty flourishes. All from the hand of a woman institutionalized at the age of sixteen.

'That's what convinced my mother – the letter with no mistakes – to move heaven and earth to find her relative. Specifically her use of the word *whom*. My mother had taught for thirty years, and she was moved to read sentences like *There are those of us for whom life is cruel and unjust.*'

She found her relation in a home in the suburbs of Toronto. A home where some fifty assorted undesirables were warehoused. The disabled, the infirm, lunatics – no distinction was made. No one wanted them. No one would claim them. They had spent their whole lives in institutions. Old and a burden, they had been parked in that house, two to a small room, with a noisy TV room and three meals a day.

I understood Bruno's anger at the rest of the story. Because that wasn't the end of it. His mother, after her first visit to her sister-in-law, took it upon herself to brighten up the woman's life. She wrote her, she sent her gifts, she called at Christmas and Easter and on her birthday, she spread kindness, talked about her special project with affection. *I just wrote to Gertrude; she's bored, the poor thing.* She enjoyed this image of herself, so kind and generous, but rejected the compliments she was paid on the matter. *It's the least I can do; it's all we can do for her now. She has lived locked away for over sixty years. She couldn't handle living any other way. It's all we can give her, a few small pleasures at the end of her life.*

Until the day when kindness and compassion were no longer enough, and she invited Gertrude to her home. Her children were now adults, and she had spare bedrooms and time to kill, but only for a few days – the poor thing couldn't stand any more.

'She just wanted something to keep her busy.'

Keeping busy, to Bruno's way of thinking, was frivolousness in its worst, most consuming form, and he believed his mother was as empty-headed as they come ...

But that was unfair. His mother had answered a plea for help that his father had ignored, and she was the one who was being criticized. It was unfair and I told him so.

'My mother just wanted something to do, to let off steam, to keep busy preparing meals and organizing a family celebration around the long-lost relative, and then when everything was done, when there was nothing left to keep her busy, so long, Gertrude. The poor lunatic was to be sent back to where she came from. Except there was a snag.'

The snag was the fiery eyes that sought out Bruno in the living room bursting with uncles, aunts, cousins and second cousins – a long sidelong look that snaked its way through the crowd and came to rest on Bruno's earlobe.

'They had all filed past her, all astonished by her excellent mental health. They were making comments and being mildly appalled. I refused to take part in the circus. But when an old woman just out of the asylum seeks you out with her eyes ... '

The dissident nephew approached his aunt, and once he leaned over her, he understood.

'It was my earring that had caught her eye.'

She pointed to his earring and told him, in a confidential tone, as if to warn him of a serious misunderstanding, 'You've made a mistake. You're a boy, not a girl,' and he, in the same tone, said, 'You're right, auntie. When I got up this morning I thought I was a girl,' and, understanding the game, she said, 'It's true. Sometimes it's hard to know what's what in the morning,' and they laughed the same laugh.

This incident and others that followed – because regularly that day they found themselves laughing at private jokes, shared flights of fancy – convinced him to stay at his mother's the whole time his aunt was there. His mother, naturally, had no idea what was going on. I understood. This woman was the only member of her species, alone on her own planet, and Bruno likes those who are unique.

'She sees things we don't see.'

But on the evening of the third day, they were no longer laughing. Her departure was set for the next morning, and she watched the preparations warily. He had not seen that look in her eye before. It was anger dug up from deep inside, sixty-six years of internment, a devil's cauldron of emotions. He felt like she was on the verge of hurling it all their faces and yet she didn't. She held back. Sixty-six years of holding back. She knew that anger was no good, that authority punished anger, and authority at this moment was the two people who were packing her suitcase; she turned her eyes, wild with the rage of impotence, to Bruno. It was to him that she said, 'I don't want to go back there.'

'That was yesterday – a century ago. What would you have done if you were in my position?'

The same thing, Bruno. I would have done the same thing, I thought. I wouldn't have let the old aunt be sent back among the headcases, but that doesn't change the fact that we have a hell of a problem here, a problem whose head is starting to seriously bob on the other side of the window.

'What about your mother?'

'Don't worry. That's my problem.'

His mother hadn't suspected a thing when he offered to make the trip to Toronto in her stead. Even he hadn't suspected a thing at that point. All he wanted was to spend a little more time with his aunt.

'That's all I was going to do, I swear, but this is how it turned out.'

As they headed south, he saw her shrink in her seat and withdraw. She became a small caged animal, and she said not a word the whole time they were driving south, and then suddenly, as if everything had already been decided without him knowing, he turned around.

'She smiled with every wrinkle on her face.'

It was then, and only then, that he realized he was heading north to bring her here, but as for the rest, what they were going to do with her, he didn't know any more than I did.

'What about your mother?' I repeated, because it seemed to me that that was a major problem.

'Don't worry about my mother. I'll handle her.'

'And the others? In Toronto, they're going to worry. They're going to call the police.'

'It's not your problem. I'm telling you, I have a plan.'

The aunt was now fully awake. I could see the white head moving from side to side, sending off its spray of light. This woman grabbed you by the heart. Her story was devastating.

We went back to the great hall where she was waiting for us, smiling like a lost child. Bruno served her a sandwich and a cup of tea and explained that she needn't worry, that he would take care of everything. Tonight she would sleep at the hotel, which he indicated with a large sweep of his hand, and tomorrow we would see about the rest.

Bruno gestured to the high ceilings, the panelled walls, the inlaid floors, the grand staircase winding above the great hall, all in varnished oak dulled by dust. The state of the place didn't make it very inviting. But that didn't seem to worry her for an instant.

We brought her to her room, the green room, the room the photographer had stayed in the week before. I wanted to whisper a word in Bruno's ear, but the thought got lost in the shuffle again.

She liked the room's silence. That's what she said: 'I like the silence in this room.'

We got her settled in with the few things from her suitcase: toiletries, drugs – lots of drugs – and a few old-fashioned articles of clothing, including a horrid purple bathrobe that Bruno, disgusted, hung in the closet.

'How about a pink terrycloth robe, would you like that, auntie?'

Pink terrycloth!

That was that. We were taking her on. Rather than being alarmed, I felt relieved, which was even more worrisome.

We left her silently contemplating her room, and we went down to the great hall where a tasty joint and a good discussion awaited us, at least that's what I thought, because on top of the issue of the aunt we had to sort out, I still hadn't said anything to Bruno about the photographer, and I wanted to talk to him about Darling, my dog.

You can't live in the forest without a dog. Ted, Charlie, Tom and I each had ours. They accompanied us, listened to us and understood us. A dog that buries its nose in your crotch when you think no one knows you exist is a familiar comfort. I've slept with Darling more than once – the nights get cold in my little cubbyhole. I've only ever slept in the office. I could have chosen a room upstairs, but I'm set in my ways. That's where I slept when the Lebanese man was here, and that's where I continued to sleep once I had the hotel all to myself.

Darling hadn't barked at the photographer's arrival. That's what worried me. She had stayed quiet, no growling or anything, and then she went to rub up against the photographer's legs and hadn't left her side all evening. That woman had a gift with dogs.

Darling was supposed to warn me when someone arrived. That's the job of any dog worth its salt, Darling even more so, because of the plantation and the old men. Ted feared nothing from anyone, historians or other worshippers of times gone by, but Tom and Charlie had left behind lives that could catch up with them. Jerry, the hotelkeeper in the next town where I went to cash their pension cheques, reminded me regularly of the illegal nature of our situation, trying to bump up his cut. But he had too much to hide himself, so I could trust him. Illegal activities get along quite nicely with the shenanigans of others. Only the pure of heart are dangerous. And the photographer, without a doubt, was one of those. What would become of us if Darling stopped barking when the pure of heart went by?

I wanted to talk about all this with Bruno. If I had known that Ted was dead, we would have talked about that too, but I didn't know. I should have known. I should have sensed his absence. Ted was our role model, our inspiration, the soul of the place. We all admired him tremendously. We knew his story. The boy who had walked through the smoking rubble. The man who appeared and disappeared. An open wound. Ted was a legend. When the Lebanese man saw him coming, he knew that the train tracks would never reach his hotel; if Mr. Boychuck had come to settle here, there was no hope for the place. He handed me the keys and went to seek his fortune elsewhere.

We smoked our joint but we didn't talk about what was on my mind. Bruno was in a rush to leave, in a rush to get to the old men's camp, in a rush to put his plan into motion – he was going to learn everything at the old men's camp.

The story takes shape quite slowly. Nothing happens very quickly north of the forty-ninth parallel. Tom and Charlie start their days by stretching their limbs, sore from sleep, and then slowly making their way to the woodstove to kindle it for the morning and potatoes with bacon. Each at their window, they study the day before them. No matter whether it's sunny or snowy, it's a nice moment, because they are able to observe it all: the snow, the wind, a rabbit's tracks, the gliding flight of a crow, life renewed – nothing they haven't seen before.

After bacon and potatoes and sweet tea comes the first cigarette, and with it, the first real thought of the day. Before that, there are only indistinct rumblings of the brain. They need a rush of nicotine to awaken their brains and make their thoughts distinguishable.

Since Boychuck's death, their first thought of the day is for their old friend. All those paintings they discovered in the locked cabin have left them with endless questions.

Charlie is on his second cigarette, and he is waiting for Tom for their morning chat. That's the way it is every day: Tom, after stoking his stove, leaves his cabin, passes in front of Ted's, stops there long enough to wonder once again at the paintings lined up like a mummified army, and continues along his path, wondering what Charlie will have to say about it – Charlie had gone there as well the evening before, at dusk. They each have their hour.

'What possessed him to leave all those paintings behind?' Tom asked.

'It's his legacy.'

'His legacy, come off it. He didn't have a woman, no children, no family. They all died in the Great Matheson Fire. Why on earth did he saddle us with them?'

'We don't have to do anything with them.'

'That doesn't stop us from thinking about them.'

'Maybe that's what he wanted.'

'What?'

'That we think about him.'

'Come on.'

Every morning, they have this conversation, or one like it, which gets them nowhere. But these are their last moments alone, just the two of them, because very soon the lakeside community will have added to its numbers the tiny old lady with the fiery eyes and the husky woman who used the pretext of the Boychuck legend to pay them a visit.

But we must pause and introduce the Great Fires that ravaged Northern Ontario at the beginning of the twentieth century.

And love? We'll have to wait a while longer. It's too soon for love.

THE GREAT FIRES

Northern Ontario was ravaged by the cruel, devastating Great Fires at the beginning of the twentieth century.

The fires were carried by violent winds over fifty, a hundred kilometres, destroying everything in their path: forests, villages, towns and lives. It was a sea of fire, a tsunami of flames that advanced with a hellish roar, impossible to flee. You had to run faster than fire, throw yourself in a lake or a river, hang on to an overloaded rowboat or a tree trunk, wait for the monster to gorge itself on its own fury, for the flames to devour one another, for nothing more to be left, for it to move on to other forests, other towns, leaving nothing behind but black, devastated earth, the smell of the end of a battle, and whatever would be discovered, or not discovered, under the ashes.

The Great Timmins Fire was the most violent. Four scorching hours and nothing was left of the small mining town. The survivors had taken refuge in Porcupine Lake. Hours of pure horror watching the flames hurl themselves at their homes, stores, the train station, all the things they had just barely finished building; the town was only two years old. But the tragedy didn't end there. The fire then headed northeast and devastated the town of Cochrane, eighty kilometres away, which had burned the previous year and would burn five years later, in 1916, during the Great Matheson Fire.

The Great Matheson Fire was the most deadly. Two hundred and forty-three souls perished. Those were the official numbers, anyway – they didn't take into account the prospectors, the trappers and the wanderers, those nameless people, with no nationality, who do not exist, who travel from place to place. This was a new frontier, and it attracted adventurers of all descriptions. A few were found in dried-up streams, but most ended up as nothing more than small piles of charred bones that the wind blew far from the accountants' figures. Five hundred dead, some said.

And then, six years after the Matheson Fire, on October 4, 1922, there was the Great Haileybury Fire, the most spectacular of the fires because it razed the county seat of the district – the only town in Northern Ontario that had a bit of sophistication. It had tramways, a cathedral, a convent, schools and a hospital, all in freestone – buildings that were thought to be fireproof and yet disintegrated like wisps of straw under the wall of flames. Only millionaire row was spared: twelve large, stately homes built by the nouveau riche of Haileybury. They had made their fortunes in the silver mines at Cobalt, a small town a few kilometres away that had burned three times in isolated fires, but that the fire, in one of those inexplicable reversals of fortune, had spared this time.

The whims of a fire cannot be explained. It can climb the highest peaks, rip the blue from the sky, spread in a reddish glow, swelling, whistling – good god, it can leap onto anything that lives, jump from shore to shore, plunge into ravines soggy with water, devour peatlands, but leave a cow grazing in a circle of grass. What is there to understand? Fire, when it achieves this power, obeys no one but itself.

Even more miraculous than the cow in a circle of grass, there were children found in a stream. The photographer heard many stories about this. At first, she didn't believe them, but people insisted. One child had been found the next day in a stream, covered in mud, but alive. 'The next day' was the part the photographer couldn't bring herself to believe. A child is a child. Having the instinct to stay submerged during the fiery storm is one thing, but to spend the entire night amid the ghosts of the inferno without panicking is unimaginable: fire leaves in its wake earth that gasps, trees that slowly burst into pieces, charred remains that crackle and whistle. How could a child wait quietly for someone to come save him when all around him monsters are stirring in the night?

The photographer heard the story of a little girl, six years old, who was entrusted with the care of two babies who were found the next day, eyes red from smoke and tears, but alive. Only the little girl had severe burns. Then there was a boy of five whose parents had handed him over to two men who were fleeing toward town in a hay wagon, believing that their child would have a better chance of making it. They managed to save their small farm, but the two men who were taking a trail barely wider than their wagon at one point believed they wouldn't make it out alive – with reason, as the trail had become a tunnel of flames. Rather than put the life of the child in danger, they left him in a stream before entering the tunnel of fire. All that was found of them was the frame of their wagon, but the child survived. His father found him the next day.

The boy's story had been told by an old woman of ninety-one. Rose Kushnir. The photographer refused to believe her until she said that she knew the boy as a young man. He survived, Rose said, but he left part of himself in that stream. He never knew how to talk to people; the words wouldn't come. It was like talking to a ghost.

Rose herself was a miracle. She and her family had survived by digging the earth between the rows of their potato field with their own hands, and they remained face down, each in their furrow, while the waves of flames rushed above them. Her mother's back and behind were burned – she had covered her youngest with her body to protect him.

The tales of the survivors were all horrific. The photographer started having nightmares. But she never gave up her quest.

Going elder to elder, she came to know the Great Fires as if she had been there herself. She encountered these old people just about everywhere. In Matheson, Timmins, Haileybury, in towns of unimaginable sadness, hamlets in the middle of nowhere, in sparkling clean hovels (the Dambrowitz sisters refused to install electricity, but played concerts, one on the piano and the other on the cello), in seniors' homes (the people she met there were practically all senile) – anywhere people talked about the Great Fires, it was with an astonished pride at having survived.

The Great Fires had their heroes and their martyrs. Boychuck was neither, but he appeared in all the tales of the survivors of the Great Matheson Fire, even in the stories of those who didn't know him, who had never seen him, who had nothing to offer on the subject. Ed Boychuck, Ted or Edward, no one could agree on his first name, was an enigmatic figure of the Great Matheson Fire. The boy who walked through the smoking rubble: that's what he was called most often.

He was fourteen years old on that hot day of July 29, 1916. A sturdy boy, not very talkative, but a good worker. He had been hired on to a team of masons who were building the home of a Matheson merchant. His family lived some ten kilometres away, and he made the trip morning and night along the railway tracks, the only real route in a land still too new to afford roads suitable for vehicles.

It was a hot, dry day. You would have thought you were in the Sahara if not for the evergreen forest spread out like an offering to the sun.

Young Boychuck was spotted all along the railway track heading toward Ramore. The fire was not yet a threat. There was smoke pretty much everywhere, but people were used to that. It was summer, bush-fire season, and smoke was just part of the landscape.

He was spotted a little later in a field. It was after noon, and the wind came up, an incredibly powerful wind that gathered the bush fires into an immense torch. The sky turned black as coal. You could hear a roar in the distance, like a locomotive barrelling full steam ahead, and by god they knew what it was! People yelled; they tried to get Boychuck's attention. Two young men hidden in a hollow wanted him to take shelter with them, but it was a waste of time because the fire overpowered their voices and the boy heard nothing, and he was no longer visible at the end of the field. It was black as night, the smoke having obliterated the sun.

People believed it was him they saw a little later on a trail not much wider than a wagon, running terror-stricken in a flash of light. He had pulled his shirt up over his head and charged into a wall of flames. This was believed to be the young Boychuck, because behind the wall of flames lay his parents' farm. But no one was sure. The man who thought he had seen him was in a pool of mud, submerged in the liquid sludge up to his mouth, and he opened his eyes just long enough to feel two burning daggers at the backs of his retinas and to forever retain the image of a boy throwing himself into the flames.

No one knows how Boychuck survived. Neither do they know whether he made it to his parents' farm, whether he saw them, his five brothers and sisters, his father, his mother, dead, all of them, asphyxiated in the root cellar, huddled up against one other, their bodies blue, frozen in a last effort to suck air through their dead, mauve lips. No one knew, because Boychuck wasn't saying. At no point in his life did he mention the fire or his roaming.

The survivor in the pond lifted himself out of his mud bed; he was covered in a thick crust of mud that flaked off as he moved, and he thought he saw Boychuck one more time, but the stabbing burn had left him half blind, and he could be sure only of a blurred shape coming down the trail with a heavy step. That man spent a month in the hospital. Patches of mud had baked into his flesh.

The stories of the first instants after the fire all mention an indefinable colour, a light emanating from the sky and the earth, the sky that had opened up once again, and the earth still burning with small fires. Blazes erupted slowly at the bases of trees and burst forth in long of gushes of sparks. The trees that were still standing were black under a blue sky and collapsed in a muffled sound, sending up thick clouds of white ash.

Golden, they wound up saying, *there was a golden light in the lull. The light of God coming for us*, they said. They all felt as though they had lived through the end of the world.

Three men waited for the angels to come to a pond. Water up to their armpits, long muddy streaks on their faces, wide dazed eyes, they thought they were the last people on earth. With them in the golden light was a moose that had also taken refuge in the pond and, perched on the shoulder of the youngest man, the one who told the story, was a bird that was chirping itself hoarse.

They saw young Boychuck go by.

He groped his way through the smoking ashes. He was covered in soot and scratches, but seemed in good shape. He was stripped to the waist. His right hand was wrapped in a rag, probably a bandage he had fashioned with what was left of his shirt.

They called out to him.

The boy passed very close by without seeing them, and they had to yell after him for him to turn and for them to see his bloodshot eyes, his vacant stare, and to understand that the boy had been struck blind.

He continued on his way as if he had heard nothing, as if he were walking in the footsteps of God himself, that's what the survivor from the pond said. He was walking like a man mired in the footsteps of a giant.

He was seen in Matheson, Nushka, Monteith, Porquis Junction, Ansonville, Iroquois Falls, and then again in Matheson, Nushka, Monteith, and again in Matheson, Nushka, until he disappeared altogether. Six days of walking aimlessly, of going round in circles. No one ever understood why. From that Saturday, July 29, when the end of the world was thought to have come, until Thursday, August 3, when a woman thought she saw him on the train taking survivors to Toronto, a good six days had passed. What had kept him wandering that way?

In Matheson, he had had his hand bandaged.

Only three houses there had withstood the fire. One of them was transformed into a dispensary. Women tore up their household linens, curtains, towels and sheets to make bandages, and goose fat canned for the winter was used as ointment.

A young girl who had grown into an old woman of ninety-three remembered the young Boychuck. She remembered him because he was wearing nothing but trousers and he didn't make a sound when they removed the rag stuck to his flesh. The palm of his hand was a bright red muscle.

In Nushka, he had a walking stick and was wearing a shirt that wasn't his own.

Nushka was a village of French-Canadian farmers some ten kilometres north of Matheson. Now it is called Val Gagné in honour of the diminutive local priest, a hero in the collective memory for having at least tried to save his congregation. Twenty-seven years old, his first parish, no experience in anything, particularly not in forest fires, he proposed to his flock, when all seemed lost, that they take refuge at the end of a clay corridor cut into a hill for the railway tracks to pass through. It wasn't such a bad idea. The corridor was set deep in the hill, the clay embankments steep, with no vegetation, so one could hope to be sheltered from the flames. But the little priest knew nothing about the workings of fire. The flames did indeed pass above the clay corridor, but they sucked out all the oxygen within it. Fifty-seven people suffocated.

The young Boychuck was seen the night of the carnage. Rain had started to fall, drizzle really, nothing that could put out an inferno but enough to cool things off a little. Did he meet Simon Aumont? Probably not. Simon Aumont was likely already unconscious in his oat field, a baby a few months old at his side, dead, while he, Simon Aumont, survived his terrible ordeal. He was working in the forest when the bomb of fire went off, and he ran to the village to help his family, finding his wife and nine children asphyxiated on the doorstep. Only the baby was still breathing, still in her mother's arms. He brought her to the oat field, believing he would find enough air in the open space, but the intense heat overcame him. He collapsed, with the baby at his side; in surviving his ordeal, Simon Aumont become a symbol of pain in Nushka, and one of the most dwelled-upon stories, the one they harped on the most, while he never wanted to breathe a word of it.

Nushka, village of the dead.

Boychuck arrived there along the railway tracks, where he stumbled upon the first of many corpses in the carnage. That's what is thought to have happened anyway, because he was found sleeping in the rain. He was taken for dead.

A woman and her two children were travelling to Monteith along the same route. They had a cow with them, the only possession they had been able to save. They were planning to get to the experimental farm in Monteith where the father worked.

The woman has long since died, but the boy, who was eight at the time, and the little girl, who was six, told the story. First, the shock of discovering bodies piled one against the other. The children thought they were sleeping. The mother knew the truth and pulled them by the hand away from the mass grave. That was when there rose in the night a long, sad monotone cry. The cow had instinctively recognized death and launched into a funereal lowing. This woke young Boychuck from among the dead.

He almost smiled, the images from a dream probably lingering, and then, feeling the rain on his face, he asked in a sleepy voice if it was over, if it was morning already.

They set off together.

This fact and the others that followed are the rare verifiable and verified parts of Boychuck's wandering, because there were other people who saw him on the evening of Saturday, July 29. They remembered the wailing cow in particular, but they did not forget the blind young man.

The days that followed the Great Fire were days spent in movement. Fathers searched for families, wives searched for husbands, children searched for parents. Young Boychuck was one wanderer among many. The legend would be formed later on, as the years and the stories went by, because the tale of the Great Fire was told for years, and in all the various accounts, one figure kept coming back: a blind boy walking through the smoking rubble.

It seems, however, that he was not blind the whole time. A man said Boychuck helped him load bodies onto a train car. Another had seen him among those unloading an aid train. And the woman who thought she had seen him on a train bound for Toronto did not mention the young man's blindness. She had noticed him because he was alone, completely alone, and staring vacantly, she said. Even though he helped some people with their luggage, he did it as if he weren't really there, as if he had left another person to act in his stead. It was this vacant stare that made him recognizable in every account and was why he was so long believed to be blind, although he had probably regained his sight gradually, fire blindness in most cases being a temporary phenomenon.

The image remained: a blind boy walking through the smoking rubble. It was fuel for stories and haunted the imaginations of survivors, and it was the founding image of the Boychuck legend.

In Matheson, where a small municipal museum does what it can to preserve the memory of the fire of 1916, there is nothing on the subject of Boychuck. Not one photo, not a single written account, nothing. But if you talk to the woman in charge of the museum, it's as if there is only one thing you need to remember: the fire forced a blind boy to walk for days to reach his beloved. Only love can explain the young man's strange behaviour – first love, the love that gives you wings and transports you beyond yourself.

The photographer listened to the woman from the museum without really believing her. There were so many stories about Boychuck, the most far-fetched of which was the one about the gold brick. In the mythology of the North, there is always a mysterious gold brick somewhere. Stolen gold, buried somewhere, and the thief, hunted by his pursuers, dies while trying to flee or comes back and cannot find his hidden treasure. There have been countless gold bricks just waiting to be dug up in Northern Ontario. Boychuck's wandering was supposedly explained as a quest for gold exposed by the fire. The photographer didn't buy it. How could a boy go off in search of gold after losing his mother and father and when all around there was nothing but death and desolation?

Maybe there was no real motivation for it. Maybe he was wandering aimlessly, suffering from fire madness, like some said, his mind paralyzed, completely overcome. It wouldn't be the first time someone faced with a wall of flames took leave of their senses. No reaction, no instinct for survival. Fire is fuelled by oxygen, taking it from the hills, from the lowlands, from wherever it passes and, before you know it, sucking the lifeblood out of the brain. Fire madness, like fire blindness, is, however, a temporary phenomenon, a few seconds, a few minutes at the most, unfortunately deadly if no one is there to shake you out of it, because after the brain is deoxygenated, it's asphyxiation or, worse, being consumed by the flames, charred.

In fact, there is something more insidious when it comes to insanity, a sort of fascination born in the spread of the flames, their strength, their omnipotence, their dazzling colours in the smoke, a horrified contemplation that continues through the race for survival and that, as the dead are counted, takes on an irrepressible need to keep moving to feel alive. Fire-crazed, that's what was said of young Boychuck. The photographer could almost believe it.

She did not believe the drivel about the flowers. He was spotted in a ravine, walking through ashes waist high, a stick in one hand and a bouquet in the other. Flowers like the sun, yellow petals and golden brown centres. Flowers for his beloved, the woman at the museum had said. The photographer let her talk.

Boychuck's wandering continued throughout his life, it seems, because he was seen again six years later, handsome and elegant in spite of his work clothes. He was part of a railway maintenance crew. Handsome and elegant, but dark and taciturn – you could pull a word out of him here and there, but never a conversation. He left after three months, came back four years later, left and then came back again, appearing and disappearing with no trace. He was known as Ted or Ed or Edward, depending on the habit his co-workers formed, never the same ones – railwaymen, carpenters, prospectors, not a single one among them claimed to be his friend. The first name changed, but that vacant stare remained.

The photographer wondered how she would manage to capture that vacancy in a photo. Those who had known him as an old man said that it was impossible to see anything in his eyes. It was like trying to read a book that had not been written. You got lost imagining what you wanted to see.

The eyes are what are most important in old people. The flesh is hanging, sagging, gathered in wrinkled knots around the mouth, eyes, nose and ears. The face is ravaged, illegible. You can't know anything about an old person unless you look into their eyes – their eyes tell the story of their lives.

If the gaze is vacant, the photo will be too, the photographer told herself.

She had photographed some hundred old people without knowing what she would do with all the photos: a book, an exhibition, she had no idea. She let herself be swept along on a quest she didn't quite understand. Her project found meaning only in the pleasure she took in meeting very old people and the history in their eyes.

All this had started one afternoon in April, two years earlier, in High Park in Toronto.

The first days of April are a blessing in Toronto. A little old lady, tiny in her blue wool coat, was getting some sun at the end of a bench under a large bare oak tree.

That patch of bright colour in the washed-out browns of the end of winter, that was what first captured the photographer's attention.

There was the deep blue of the coat, the magenta of the beret, the white curls that escaped it, a dazzling white, and around the rim of the beret and at its centre, an embroidering of silver beads that sparkled in the sunlight. At the lady's feet was a large canvas bag with Moorish patterns, and on one end of the bench was a square of cotton in yellow and red plaid with balls of crustless bread laid out on it, which she was feeding to the birds.

The photographer took a spot at the other end of the bench and watched her discreetly.

She was very old, wizened to the bone, and there was something unresolved in her, as if she were carried along by an infinite number of thoughts that scattered in the air while she fed the pigeons. She moved methodically and slowly. When her square of cotton was empty, she would draw a hunk of bread from her bag, remove the soft part and form balls that she placed in tight rows on the square of cotton.

The photographer didn't dare take her picture. She should have. There was a pink light that sparkled at the corner of her eyes.

She didn't remember how she struck up a conversation or how they came to talk about the Great Fires.

The little old lady was a survivor of the Great Matheson Fire. She told her about the sky black as night and the birds that were falling from it like flies.

'It was raining birds,' she told her. 'When the wind came up and covered the sky with a dome of black smoke, the air was in short supply, and you couldn't breathe for the heat and the smoke, neither the people nor the birds, and they fell like rain at our feet.'

The conversation wended its way with their thoughts. The swamp white oaks that populated High Park, the still reticent spring, the noises of the city that reached them occasionally, back to the Great Fires, litter on the park paths, the end of civility, and again the Great Fires.

'When the flames reached the sky,' she had said, 'it was as if we were swimming at the bottom of a sea of fire.'

Images that the photographer committed to memory.

But the little old lady was going to leave. Her stores of bread were depleted and the daylight was fading. She was going to leave without the photographer knowing anything about her, not even her name, and as if it were the only thing to know, as one would do with a child, she asked her age.

'One hundred and two,' the little old lady said, and her eyes twinkled with mischief.

She had pulled herself up from the bench by leaning on her cane and walked straight ahead, leaving the photographer stunned. Was she really one hundred and two?

It was all there, the twinkle of pink light in the eyes of an old lady who was having a little fun with her age and the image of birds raining down from a black sky. It all started there. The photographer would not have ventured out along Northern roads, would not have thrown herself into this quest, if she had taken a picture at that moment, if she had snapped the birds raining down in the eyes of the little old lady in High Park.

Enticed and intrigued by a little old lady who had images of such destructive beauty locked inside her, and then enticed and intrigued by all the old people whose heads were filled with the same images.

She had come to love them more than she would have believed. She loved their worn-out voices, their ravaged faces; she loved their slow gestures, their hesitation before a word that escaped them, a memory that wouldn't come; she loved seeing them set themselves adrift in the currents of their thoughts and then, in the middle of a sentence, doze off. Old age seemed to her to be the ultimate refuge of freedom, where one releases oneself of any bonds and lets one's mind wander at will.

She had met all the known survivors of the Great Fires. Boychuck was to be the last.

'Dead and buried,' Charlie had said. 'Just reached his expiration date,' Tom had told her.

The legend of the Great Matheson Fire was no longer of this world. She was not terribly surprised. It wouldn't be the first time that she had knocked at the door of someone who had died the day before, the day before that, or ages ago. Nor was she overly saddened or disappointed. Tom and Charlie were worth the trip. The two laughing hermits were rare specimens in her collection of old folks. She was determined to return to their hideaway. To take pictures or for the pleasure of conversation, no matter – her quest had long ago gone beyond a photo project.

Tom and Charlie are on their fifth cigarette. The morning's conversation lingers awhile on whether Ted knew it was his time, if he had seen death coming or if she had taken him by surprise.

Death is an old friend. They talk about her casually. She has been on their heels for so long that they can feel her presence lurking, waiting, discreet during the day but sometimes intrusive at night. Their morning conversation is one way of keeping her at bay. Once they have said her name, she arrives, joins in their conversation, won't relent, wanting the spotlight, and they snub her, make fun of her, at times insult her and then send her off, and she, like a good dog, goes back to gnawing her bone in her corner. She's in no rush.

Charlie is the authority when it comes to death. He got to know her up close while he waited for her in his trapping camp. And Tom never stops asking him, 'Did you see her? Did you see her?'

'No, I didn't see her. It wasn't my time.'

'So tell me, why didn't you take your pinch of salt then? It would have been so simple.'

'I'm telling you, it wasn't my time. Plus, it was summer, it was warm, and there was a sweet smell in the air, I heard the birds chirping – it wasn't my time.'

'Methinks, dear Charlie, that it will never be your time. That you'll never decide.'

Soon they would stop having these private conversations in Charlie's cabin. Great change was coming to the little community by the lake.

THE COMMUNITY BY THE LAKE

Great change was coming to the little community by the lake. The idea of a woman, not to mention an old, very fragile woman, in a place so rugged was quite simply inconceivable. And yet the idea of that inconceivable female presence was taking shape. No one had said it, but they all knew they wouldn't let the woman go back to where she came from. In this community, there was a strong enough spirit of revolt and bravado to tackle the impossible. But how?

Bruno had quickly sorted things out with his mother. He called her from a service station to tell her that his aunt had escaped when he went to pay for gas in Huntsville – he had looked for her everywhere, but to no avail. He had waited for the police, answered their questions, signed a statement and returned, reassured by the polite indolence. They would only take so far the search to find an old woman nobody wanted.

So now she found herself expelled from the world, completely dependent on them, and they would have to solve some problems the situation posed, the first being to house her in a modicum of comfort. Ted's cabin offered this minimal comfort, but they were reluctant. It was as if Ted still lived there.

Marie-Desneige, who was still named Gertrude, had grown accustomed to her room, left it rarely and didn't seem to worry what would become of her. Her current preoccupation was choosing a new name for herself. She was torn between those of the residents of 999 Queen Street she had known, and there had been many. She also felt like inventing one. It was an amusing pastime, absorbing, an honour and a responsibility that left her no time for anything else. She wrote each name on a piece of paper so as not to forget it, and annotated it so as not to forget the person who went by that name. It seemed to her that the world was laid out before her when she spread all the pages on the bed.

She had been there for four days and nothing had been decided, neither in the great hall where Bruno and Steve smoked their brains out nor on the shores of the lake. And yet the old woman would have to live somewhere other than the Lebanese man's hotel. Fall was on the way and with fall the hunters, the transients and other askers of questions.

On the morning of the fifth day, they decided to bring her to the old men's camp to see how things would go on either side. The trip was made on a quad. Once again, she showed no surprise. Not even when she had to get up on this strange machine and wrap her arms around Bruno. Steve followed on foot accompanied by his dog.

Tom and Charlie, alerted by the noise, were waiting for them outside.

There was a crowd in front of Charlie's cabin. Four men, one woman, four dogs and a cloud of mosquitoes that had come to greet them all.

Tom, as was his habit, was showing off. He greeted the lady and added a wink that, he thought, would make any woman in good working order blush. He tried to blush himself when he realized that he would have to apologize to the lady, but at his age the blood doesn't really rush anywhere, and he contented himself with staying pale and thinking that this woman was too pretty, a finely cut gem, too pretty and too graceful, and she didn't belong among them.

Charlie went about his duties as host so as not to have to

say anything. He found everyone a comfortable log, lit the fire to chase away the mosquitoes and disappeared into his cabin to heat the water while mentally counting the receptacles he had for tea. The old lady, with her lather of hair and hands like lace, was as delicate as a fledgling. It seemed all it would take would be to blow on her for the fledgling to tumble from her seat. The thought bothered him. Rather than blowing on her, he wanted to take the baby bird in the hollow of his hand and bring her back to the nest, a thought that bothered him even more.

Steve and Bruno led the conversation, exchanging thoughts on the nice weather and trout fishing, while waiting for the opportunity to slide toward what was on their minds.

The tea was finished, the sun was reaching its zenith, and they still hadn't taken a first step toward what seemed to be an impossible objective: convincing themselves that the aunt could stay in Ted's cabin.

That's when Charlie first spoke.

'What should we call you?' he asked.

And the aunt answered immediately, as if her response had been prepared, even though she was still wondering which name to choose among all the ones she had left on her bed.

'Marie-Desneige.'

'Marie-Desneige. That's a nice name.'

Without realizing it, Charlie had just accepted Marie-Desneige's presence among them. As a result, his mind starting moving very fast, faster than he was used to, too fast, the ideas bumping into one another, so that he couldn't follow them all, and he heard himself say, even before the idea had taken shape in his mind:

'We'll build you something, not too far, something comfortable, here, next to my cabin. We can't let you live as if you've spent your whole life in the woods.'

It was unexpected, disconcerting, but entirely feasible. The idea quickly made its home in each of them, so relieved were they not to have to disturb Ted in his spirit life. And the idea was exciting. They hadn't built a cabin since Tom's. There had been a few sheds that had collapsed and had to be rebuilt, but a cabin to live in, that was something different entirely. A cabin to live in, well, it was where you lived, and where you died. It was where you saw the sun waiting for you on summer mornings and set in winter. It was where you heard noises in the night. A cabin to live in was your companion in all of your thoughts. With a cabin to live in, you were never alone.

Something comfortable, Charlie had said, and he was right. The lady, Marie-Desneige, needed a cabin with all the modern conveniences. Running water, they quickly agreed, she needed running water. No small order. They discussed it at length. And then they decided that she would also need an indoor shower and toilet. More technical problems that they seized on enthusiastically. Building Marie-Desneige's cabin absorbed them to the point that they forgot about its future occupant, sitting on her stump, looking, distraught, from one to the other.

'A cat. I would like a cat in my house.'

A feeling of discomfort and relief among the men. She had just called them up short on their bad manners by reminding them she was there, but had indicated her consent to it all so long as a cat was thrown in.

They built her a cabin next to Charlie's. All the mod cons: running water, indoor shower and toilet, which required major work. The water was brought up from the lake by a pipe wrapped in insulation and pumped indoors by a gas generator. They would use propane to heat the water for the shower, to provide light and heat and to power the fridge and stove – luxury items in the deep woods but deemed necessary for a lady who was used to neither firewood nor maintaining a home. She appeared to be capable of nothing. Sixty-six years of institutionalization had left her with no skills or bearings. A baby bird who had fallen from the nest, Charlie thought once again.

The work took three weeks. The cabin took shape fairly quickly because they had opted for a traditional structure with beams and insulating boards. A log cabin would have taken too much time. The cabin had a main room and in the back, on the north side, a tiny room that they called the bathroom. They were so impressed, Tom and Charlie in particular, who had long forgotten these conveniences, that they wound up dispensing with the term *cabin*, referring instead to Marie-Desneige's *little house*.

The work started early in the morning with Steve and Marie-Desneige's arrival on a quad. Marie-Desneige loved her room, but could no longer stand being alone at the hotel, and although she was of no use whatsoever at the construction site, she spent her days there. Bruno arrived later. He had traded in his van for a pickup truck, loaded with everything needed for the work. Money wasn't a problem, and had never been – the plantation provided more than was necessary.

Marie-Desneige's mood started to show cracks as the days went by. At first it was just tiny flickers in her eyes, and then dark areas, and then she disappeared, her eyes went empty.

Sometimes they would hear her singing. She would go sit in the grass near the lake and stay there a long time, absorbed, they thought, in contemplating the water. A voice would rise softly, very different from the one they were used to her using. A pure, crystalline voice, light and distant. Only a few flutey notes would reach them over the hammering. They would slow their pace, and the melody would spread its wings.

It was a song of ancient times, the son of a king who loved a shepherdess, the farewells of a man going to the gallows, a sad story that Marie-Desneige sang in a tender voice. She sang it in a loop, once, twice, three times, the voice growing hoarse at the saddest part of the story, six times, eight times, the voice trailing off to nothing more than a murmur, nine times, ten times, the hammers falling silent, all eyes turning toward the lake. Marie-Desneige, her knees hugged against her, was rocking back and forth and mumbling a song, its pain reaching them in muted notes of despair.

The incantatory songs at the edge of the lake made them worry that insanity was slowing resurfacing.

The work continued, and Marie-Desneige's quarters were ready in early September. A small house just slightly larger than Charlie's cabin, with screens on the windows, black lathing paper on the outside walls and a sheet-metal roof that overhung the doorway. They imagined that this part jutting out could become a screened-in porch where Marie-Desneige would rock on summer evenings singing her sad melodies. The insanity might be just that, too much sadness. She simply needed some space.

The day finally arrived when Marie-Desneige moved into her house. A grey day, overcast, and a little rain holding back. The furniture was moved in hastily and haphazardly, furniture Bruno had procured from different places so as not to arouse curiosity, bought ready made; there was no question of fashioning a table with an axe for Marie-Desneige. No time and out of the question – Marie-Desneige needed things nice and new. A table, three chairs, a box spring, a mattress, a gas stove and a small refrigerator, all of which were stored in the great hall of the hotel and then loaded into the pickup, transferred to the quad trailer and hauled into the little house.

The photographer appeared at the end of the trail just as they were fussing around the refrigerator.

They had forgotten about her.

Charlie noticed her first, surrounded by dogs and waving something over her head.

The photos of Chummy, he thought. How could I forget she was coming back with them?

It was indeed the pictures of Charlie's dog that she was waving about. A pretty flimsy calling card under the circumstances.

In a single movement, the four men gathered in front of the door to stop her from going in and, above all, to hide Marie-Desneige in case she felt like going out. But it was like trying to hold back the rain. Sooner or later in the next few minutes, the photographer's questions would come, and nothing they could answer would turn things around.

There was a lot of brain activity in the compact, hostile mass that greeted the photographer. Steve was fuming at the dogs for not announcing her arrival. The woman truly has a gift, he thought. Bruno was thinking that she wasn't bad at all, this woman, hefty but in the right proportions, and, well, almost pretty. The thought shone in his eyes, which did not escape Tom, who was amusing himself with the idea of romance. Charlie dropped the idea of driving the intruder away with a few shotgun shots, but, lips sealed, he thought, I won't say a word, she'll get nothing out of me.

All of this would prove to be pointless.

When Marie-Desneige heard the photographer's voice greet the men, it awoke something in her, a memory, a hope, something pleasant, absolutely irresistible, because she swept out of the house, made a beeline through the men and found herself all smiles before the photographer.

'Ange-Aimée,' she whispered.

They were witnessing the ebbing of her old life, someone she thought she recognized, a person who had been dear to her, probably a friend who had been through the bad and the unimaginable at her side.

'Ange-Aimée,' she whispered again, but sadly. The voice was barely audible, the disappointment palpable.

They grieved for her, they wanted to console her. The men were caught off guard faced with a woman's distress, but the photographer knew what to do. She leaned toward Marie-Desneige, took her hands and brought them to her lips.

'You can call me Ange-Aimée if you like.'

Marie-Desneige's smile returned tentatively.

The photographer had just won Marie-Desneige's friendship and, along with it, her admission to the hideaway. They didn't realize it at the time. It was only afterward, when Marie-Desneige led the photographer into the house and they heard laughing and chattering, that they understood that their little community would never be the same.

The two women finally came out, and the photographer announced that Marie-Desneige would need sheets, towels and curtains.

Curtains!

And just like that, it was done. There were two women at the hideaway. One there to live and the other, the visitor, free to come and go. And they were left powerless before these two women and a burgeoning friendship.

They did what they were told and brought linens, dishes and other household necessities from the hotel, but not curtains because the ones at the hotel fell apart in their hands. Tomorrow, I'll go buy curtains, the photographer decided, and the day ended on this solemn promise.

And just like that, Marie-Desneige was settled in her house for the night. She had unpacked her suitcase, hung up her clothes, put on her nightdress and was waiting in her bed, her hands flat on her thighs and her back straight, waiting for her body to slowly come back together again. All day she had felt as though it wanted to get away from her. First there was that feeling of cold in her lungs which had moved to her stomach, and then the cold had disappeared, she no longer felt it. She felt nothing further where the cold had passed, and it was terrifying, because she knew that she was slowly starting to disintegrate. This feeling of her body dissolving was familiar to her – she had had to battle it her whole life. The medication had helped, but she had run out, her supply was exhausted, and it took tremendous concentration to restore her bodily integrity.

A song rose up in the night. The wind had dropped, and the forest was dark and silent. The only thing that could be heard was the whispering trees. Marie-Desneige's song rose up, and the night carried her prayer up to the endless skies.

Charlie was on watch. He waited until he could no longer see any lights in her little house before going to bed. He smoked and drank tea, wondering whether Marie-Desneige understood how to operate the propane lamp.

The song reached him just as he was about to go outside, convinced she needed help turning off the lamp.

It was an old sea shanty, slow and weighed down with thwarted love, that spread its lament over a melody smelling of spring tides, salty sea spray and pitching on rough waters. A melody that after having come around a number of times becomes more bitter, more laboured, scraping the bottom of merciless seas. Charlie wanted to hear it no more, but the song went back to the beginning, the sailor boarded the ship again, his heart heavier, and poured out his misfortunes into a bottomless sea. Charlie couldn't take it anymore. He wanted it to stop, he wanted her done with all this misfortune that was not her own, but she revelled in it, immersed herself in it. She was the sailor who had sailed the world's seas seeking oblivion. The song took on a more intimate pain, the voice forgot itself, got lost, dropped to no more than a whisper in the night, and Charlie knew that Marie-Desneige over there, so near, in the little house, in her bed, was rocking back and forth holding her body close as if she were rocking a doll.

Marie-Desneige was indeed rocking her body while quietly singing it the final verses of her sea shanty. She hoped it would come back to her. A number of times she had managed to bring her body back together this way. This time there was resistance, something stopping it, an opposing force that warded off her lament, and she thought it was the house, too new, too lonely. She had never slept with no one nearby, with no one in the same room.

When Charlie heard a sound at his door, he knew who was on the other side.

She had put on a coat over her nightgown. In the moonlight, her hair was a dazzling sight, and in the dark of the night her eyes conveyed her immense distress.

'Can I sleep here?'

With a sweep of his hand, he gestured to the bed of pelts that awaited her.

They each have their own corner, Marie-Desneige in her nest of furs and Charlie on his mattress at the other end of the room. But since the cabin is small and the night silent, they can hear each other move, they can hear each other breathe. Charlie can barely stand the intimacy. He isn't used to sharing the night with anyone but Chummy. And then the silence that grows heavier when sleep doesn't come. Charlie figures he has to ask a question to lift the weight, but what should he ask?

'Was Ange-Aimée a friend of yours?'

'She was the queen of our ward. Everyone respected her. She walked like a queen, talked like a queen, and I was her friend. Her lady's maid.'

'Her lady's maid?'

They are whispering more than speaking. Charlie is using his velvety voice, the one he uses to approach a frightened animal. Marie-Desneige is more and more at ease. She is used to dormitories, secrets whispered between beds. Using a hushed voice, barely audible, she recounts some of her life in the asylum with her friend who believed she was the queen of Scotland and who gave her stockings to wash and hems to mend in exchange for her protection.

'Nobody would have dared take on Ange-Aimée, Queen of Scotland, England, the Carpathians and the United Nations.'

'The Carpathians isn't a country.'

'Neither is the United Nations.'

They laugh, amused at having thought almost the same thing at the same time, surprised to find themselves on common ground.

'And why Marie-Desneige?'

'There were a lot of Marys. Mary Lynn, Mary Ann, Mary Beth, Marie-Louise, Mary Kate, Mary Margaret, Mary Jane

and just plain Mary. But there was only one Marie-Desneige. She was the prettiest one.'

'It's a nice name.'

This is said in a goodnight tone, and indeed, they say nothing further and fall asleep.

CHARLIE'S THIRD LIFE

The photographer finally had a name. She would be called Ange-Aimée, the name of the Queen of Scotland and the Carpathians who ruled over the lunatics – no matter that she already had a name. Marie-Desneige decided how things would be, without really meaning to or realizing it.

Life in the lakeside community revolved around Marie-Desneige's needs, whether expressed or not. She got her cat and her curtains, and the photographer as a friend. The cat was a two-year-old male tabby that she called Monseigneur; the curtains had a dainty floral pattern, a pale salmon pink, that brightened up the house both inside and out; and her friend Ange-Aimée went from the royal protector she had been in another life to become her lady's companion.

Marie-Desneige was adjusting wonderfully to her new life. She had learned how to handle propane, could peel potatoes without cutting her hands and studied the colour of the sky every morning, but being alone in her house with no one around, that she couldn't handle. Charlie realized this one day when he came back from hunting and discovered her in his cabin, buried under the bundle of furs, her body wearily rocking and, in her eyes, the desperate struggle of an animal in a trap.

Ange-Aimée the photographer became a necessary presence, both to keep the demons away and to find in stores what had become indispensable: slippers, a nightgown, a knitting kit and novels to fill the evenings, romances mainly, and now that winter was coming, even more novels.

The green room was assigned to her as a matter of course, even though she regularly returned to Toronto where she had an apartment, her darkroom and all the photos that waited for her to decide their fate. The Great Fires, Boychuck and his mystery, all of this was dim and distant now that there was this little old woman on the lam trying to make a life at the end of the world with two men even older than her.

'I always knew I would have a life,' Marie-Desneige said to Ange-Aimée in the early days of their friendship. 'I never gave up hope of having a life of my own.' And Ange-Aimée the photographer, deeply moved to be witnessing the dawn of a new life, slipped into another skin.

A bit like when a newborn arrives in a family, a sort of grace descended upon the community and ensured there were no concerns other than the well-being of the new arrival. The most apparent change, even though no one took notice of it, was that they stopped talking about death. The subject had been lost in the shuffle of settling Marie-Desneige in, and then in the fun of discovery. She had seen her first flock of Canada geese, her first hare tracks in the snow, a moose that came to drink from the lake, an owl in the bare arms of a birch – everything was new and fresh to Marie-Desneige's eyes.

Death held no interest. They no longer talked about her, didn't even think about her. They were in the presence of a new life spreading its wings.

But their old friend still lurked, no matter what they wanted to believe, and sometimes she took advantage of their inattention to slip into a conversation that had nothing to do with her. For instance, there was the snow, not yet very deep but staying on the ground. Winter was definitely pressing to settle in. They would probably need more firewood than last year. They were wondering whether they would dip into Ted's wood supply. And Marie-Desneige wanted to know who Ted was. While they were explaining, death breathed easily. She had reasserted herself. But not for long. Boychuck was of greater interest alive than dead.

Through a strange conversational detour one day, death managed to fix their attention on Charlie's salt box enthroned on the shelf above his bed. Ange-Aimée, because that's what she had to be called, was at the hideaway for a few days and had brought from Toronto an enormous Italian cake that was so heavy and sweet they had to sample it in small mouthfuls. There was no reason for any interest in the salt box. It was on its shelf, and they were around the table, eating the terribly sweet cake. There are only so many ways to explain what happened. Only a malignant presence, lurking somewhere at the far end of the cabin, frustrated and vengeful, could have forced their eyes toward the tinplate box after Tom, for no reason, made this reflection about the overly sweet cake.

'It's so good, I think I'll go without salt today, Charlie my boy.'

All eyes, including those of Marie-Desneige and Ange-Aimée, who knew nothing about anything, turned toward the box. Somebody had to explain it. It was Charlie who did.

Instinctively, he had spotted death's presence and set out to chase her off. He explained that the box contained a medicine of last resort. 'There is no doctor or hospital here,' he said, 'and there are limits to what a person can endure.' A flash of panic passed through Marie-Desneige's eyes. 'Nobody here wants to die,' he hastened to add, 'but nobody wants a life that is no longer his own either.' Marie-Desneige closed her eyes. How long had she been imprisoned in a life that was not her own, how many years had been stolen from her? Charlie had to be aware of the thoughts raging behind Marie-

Desneige's closed eyelids. 'And that,' he said, pointing to the tinplate box, 'is what makes the sunset worthwhile when our bones are aching, that's what gives us the desire to live, because we know we have a choice. The freedom to live or to die, there's nothing like it to make you choose life.'

So there. It was said. They wouldn't revisit the topic. The cabin breathed more freely. Death could forget about it. It would stay relegated to the shadows for the time being. The conversation then latched on to something more substantial, because Tom started to tell Charlie's story to convince Marie-Desneige, in case she had any doubt left, that no one here wanted to die. 'This stubborn old mule brought his salt box here out of pure bravado,' Tom said, gesturing to Charlie.

'This is my first life,' Marie-Desneige said, 'and I'm hanging on to it.'

Many other conversations followed this one. Winter would soon cover the forest with her icy stillness. The only place for a little entertainment was around the fire, and that winter was particularly entertaining. Conversations had never been so lively. They revealed a Marie-Desneige braced, determined to live the life that had been given to her, outraged, deeply outraged – her life had been stolen from her, she often repeated.

These conversations generally took place at Charlie's. They involved the three elders and sometimes Ange-Aimée. It wasn't unusual to see Bruno and Steve arrive on a Skandic. If there were six in Charlie's little cabin, they would move to Marie-Desneige's, her house being larger and already equipped with three chairs. They just had to bring two chairs and the metal pail from Charlie's to seat everyone.

There were memorable moments. Like the time Bruno brought Chinese food from a restaurant in a neighbouring town. Six aluminum dishes filled to the brim with fried rice, stir-fried vegetables, garlic spare ribs and breaded shrimp. Two hundred kilometres there and back. The dishes were cold. They put them in the oven and they came out bubbling, steaming and fragrant. They talked about it for days.

The winter was particularly cold, hard and brazen. It stung the nostrils as soon as you stuck your nose outside. Tom had a flu that kept him in bed for two weeks. Ange-Aimée was the nurse. Charlie spent his days at Marie-Desneige's. The sound of the nails in her house exploding in the cold terrified her. Steve and Bruno handled the rest, checking the hare traps, drilling holes in the ice, carrying water and firewood. They took care of everything because Tom was still weak from the flu and Marie-Desneige was scared by the noises in her house.

The lakeside community grew closer over the winter, huddled together in the heart of the deep cold, never very far from one another. Marie-Desneige blossomed like a young girl under all the attention. There were no more incantatory songs to make your blood run cold. She was still haunted by irrepressible fears, the worst being the feeling that her body was slipping away from her. And every evening, fearing that that horrible thing would happen again, she would knock at Charlie's door.

She didn't spend a single night in her own home. She was used to dormitories, she explained to Charlie, was used to falling asleep under the thick odour of a dormitory, twenty women around her, their warm breath, the weight of their dreams intermingled and, close by, in the bed next to her, her friend Ange-Aimée.

Charlie would be waiting for her. He would have unrolled the pelts and filled the stove with dry birch logs, waiting for the shiver that would let him know the precise moment she knocked at the door.

She would arrive wrapped in her coat, her eyes pleading with him to protect her from herself. All she had on under her coat was her nightgown, a thing of wonder in Charlie's eyes, a nightgown in white flannelette lit up at the neck with pink trim, the only feminine clothing he had seen in a dog's age, as the two women at the camp covered themselves during the day in thick shirts over their men's pants.

Marie-Desneige would go straight to her bed and slide under the furs. Charlie waited until then to turn out the light. He would not have greeted Marie-Desneige in Stanfield's, the long wool underwear that covered his whole body and never left it in the winter, not even to sleep, a second skin, as fragrant as the first one but smooth and uniformly grey. So he waited to be in the dark to strip down to his Stanfield's and slide under the covers in turn.

Chummy, during the depths of the cold of winter, was also in the cabin. Stretched out on his side in the middle of the room, he formed a sort of rampart, an invisible barrier that allowed them to believe they were protected from too much intimacy. They could talk without worrying what would come to mind because they were in the dark, at a distance from one another, and would soon be submerged in a sleep that would wipe away all that had been said. Everything was in place for the long conversations that acted as a lullaby, Marie-Desneige falling asleep first and Charlie waiting for this moment to slip out of bed and put another birch log on the fire.

Their nighttime conversations found no echo the next day. The first up, Charlie fed the stove, boiled the water for the tea and set about preparing breakfast. Marie-Desneige got up in turn and came to help him. An old couple, Charlie sometimes thought, and it surprised him each time that this thought did not turn his mind to the woman he had left fifteen years before.

The first time Tom discovered them this way, he felt as though he had walked in on an old couple in the middle of their morning routine. Marie-Desneige in her nightgown, Charlie dressed, but his bed unmade, and the bed of pelts spread out nicely in the other corner of the room. There was no doubt about it; they had spent the night together.

Well, Charlie my boy ...

He'd arrived, as was his custom, for his morning chat with Charlie and discovered him shacked up, as it were. He could have felt insulted, betrayed or dispossessed. These morning conversations had been something exclusive, a ritual they never missed. And here was his companion alone with a woman in a nightgown. But twisted feelings didn't last long in the forest – it would have made survival impossible. Tom sat down at the table in calm uncertainty, waiting for his inner turmoil to subside to find the right thing to say.

He got used to seeing them together. When she was not at his place, he was at hers, or they headed out together through the deep snow to observe the signs of a spring that was taking its time in coming. She, so tiny and fragile, a little bird always on the verge of being carried off by a wind of panic, and him, large, so heavy and so slow, a block of granite that it seemed nothing could shake.

All he had to do was lay his hand where she showed him and she would resurface. There, she would say. It was the lungs or the stomach or the liver, an organ was cold and was in danger of disappearing. Charlie's hand slowly, gently filled the gap, and Marie-Desneige, serene again, smiled at the life that had returned to her.

An old bear holding an ethereal creature down to earth. *Methinks you're beginning a third life, Charlie my boy.*

It is cold in Charlie's cabin. There is a full moon. The cold is sharp and biting. The stove barely manages to sustain a circle of lukewarmth, which fails to reach the corners of the cabin.

From his bed, Charlie observes with concern the cloud of condensation escaping from the nest of furs. He wants her to burrow into the warmth, but he knows that Marie-Desneige won't sleep until she finishes telling the story she has started.

'The first time, I thought someone else had come to inhabit me. I believed it was an angel, a celestial being who had taken over my body. I thought I was going to start to fly. I didn't panic. It was real and yet unreal. Like a game. I left my body where it was, and I went to tell my mother that I had become an angel.'

Marie-Desneige tries to explain the process of becoming disembodied that she has suffered from since adolescence.

'They put me away. I was sixteen years old.'

Charlie is concerned.

'I don't feel like there is a foreign presence anymore, or an angel, or a being from the great beyond. There's just me and a feeling of emptiness. It's very real, but it's hard to explain. It's very slow at first, vague, the sensation of an emptiness that is trying to find a place. I can see exactly where it begins. In the organs, often around the liver. When the emptiness settles in, it sucks up all the rest. Leaving is easy, but coming back is dreadful. It's the memory of that horror that terrifies me as soon as I feel the emptiness attack me.'

Charlie isn't worried for the part of Marie-Desneige that is tucked under the furs. He knows how warm her cozy little nest is. He has often slept in it with Chummy. What worries him is the white, luminous spot, Marie-Desneige's head outside the nest, the condensation escaping from it that has now formed a little white cloud. It's getting colder.

'Tell me about Ange-Aimée.'

He hopes she will fall asleep telling the story told many times before and that she will burrow down further in the furs.

'When we met, I was seventeen and she was twenty-one. It was major nervous exhaustion that had brought her there after her first baby, the only one she ever had. They had labelled her with a diagnosis of progressive melancholia and gave her a hysterectomy. She was in a sorry state when I met her. She spent all day rocking in the day room with a phantom baby in her arms. My diagnosis was premature dementia, because of how I would see my body disintegrate. Then they said it was schizophrenia.

'I rocked her baby. That's how we became friends. I asked her if I could rock her baby. She passed him to me very carefully, and I took him just as carefully, and I rocked the baby too, for a long time, singing songs to him. And that's how, taking turns rocking a baby that didn't exist, we figured out how not to be where we were. We rocked the baby for a year, and then he died. We had a funeral for him, and Ange-Aimée became the queen of Scotland and England. The Carpathians and the United Nations came later. It saved our lives. For years, we reigned over ourselves. We didn't see the rats or the cockroaches. We couldn't hear the cries or the howls. We had our own world, our own laws, our own fantasies. She was my queen and I was her lady's maid. My body held fast. Sometimes I would see it go off, but I would hang on and it would come back.'

'Are you cold?'

He doesn't want to hear the rest. He doesn't want her to tell the story. The separation, the electric shock, the insulin comas – he can't handle the rest anymore. They were separated. Their friendship was thought to be wicked. Wicked for whom, wicked why, when you were a patient at 999 Queen Street – these were questions you didn't ask. Ange-Aimée was transferred to the manic floor, and hell began for Marie-Desneige. The panic attacks intensified. Her body disappeared without warning, sometimes completely. Electric shock, insulin comas – she was subjected to every psychiatric horror of the time. She doesn't know how she escaped a lobotomy. Nor does she know what became of Ange-Aimée. She never saw her again.

'No, you're the one who's cold.'

From her cozy nest, she hears him toss and turn in his bed, seeking warmth. The cold cuts like a knife. The stove does its best, but nights with a full moon are cruel. Charlie gets up regularly to feed the fire. She knows he won't sleep, that he will watch over the fire all night.

'Come over here. It's warm here. You're freezing in that bed.'

The invitation is tempting. He is familiar with the enveloping warmth of fur. But sleeping alongside Marie-Desneige, close to a woman, he can't. His body refuses. It would be letting go too much.

He gets up to feed the stove again and the feeling of his body being cut to the quick by the cold finally drives him to Marie-Desneige's bed.

'You see. That wasn't so hard,' she says, opening up her bed to him, and he stretches out at her side, the frost of their breath meeting in a little white cloud that gets lost in the night.

Chummy comes to join them.

Their first night in the nest of pelts.

YOUNG GIRLS WITH LONG HAIR

Spring took a long time coming. The ice on the lake didn't break up until mid-May, and it wasn't until the beginning of June that you could really feel comfortable. There were still patches of snow in the forest. The north wind snatched shivers from you even in the sun.

In mid-June, the ground seemed ready to receive the first marijuana plants. The seedlings had been cluttering up the hotel's kitchen for a whole month already. They had to be planted before they started to wilt. The plantation was on the side of a hill, near Tom's camp. The operation was not very complicated but it required a few days' work, which meant that Marie-Desneige and Ange-Aimée were alone at the camp while the men tended to their plantation.

Ange-Aimée had long ago figured out what was going on. The lack of concern for money, the fat joints that Steve and Bruno passed back and forth at the hotel, the bags of fertilizer piled up in the kitchen: it was more than enough evidence for a woman of the world.

As for Marie-Desneige, she didn't understand it. They explained it to her over and over, but nothing stuck. It was beyond her comprehension. Cigarettes that you smoke to escape reality, to travel in your head, as they said, without suitcases or landmarks? She couldn't understand why sane people would want to dabble in madness.

So the two women had a few days, which they spent in

long walks. Everything was in bloom. Summer was eager to make its appearance, and the two women followed the trails that took them to a cascading stream, and further down, a spawning bed for pike, and further still, a patch of tiny violets, *northern woodland violets,* Ange-Aimée said, remembering her other life. *They're edible. You can make jam with them,* and so the two women crouched down in the undergrowth.

They visited Tom's camp, a dump that defied words, and passed Ted's camp a number of times before convincing themselves they could take a peek. The winter's conversations had made it a mythical, almost sacred, place – at the very least, forbidden. No one had been inside it since the previous summer, and so it was with a great deal of caution, marked with curiosity and respect, that they entered Ted's cabin.

Ange-Aimée, with her photographer's eye, quickly spotted the canvasses, intrigued. There was nothing naïve or clumsy in them, as she had imagined. There was a thick sfumato shot through with black lines, behind which you could detect the presence of a true artist. Under the smoky grey, stains of colour that came together in an arborescence encircled with an indigo-blue line. The three canvasses repeated the same composition. The one on the easel was more fraught with emotion. The canvas was lit in its centre with a depth that the others did not have.

'They're dead, all of them, and there are lots of people in the cave,' Marie-Desneige said.

'What? What did you say?'

'There are six of them, maybe more, the pink spot inside the orangey splotch. It could be someone smaller, a child perhaps, a very young child, probably a baby, and they're all dead. Look at how the blue around them is hard and cold. Maybe the orangey splotch is pregnant actually, the mother hasn't given birth yet. The pink spot is a child waiting to be born or a very young baby in the arms of its mother, and there is nothing moving in the cave.'

A cellar, not a cave, the root cellar where Ted's father, mother and five brothers and sisters had died. The only point she had wrong was the cave. As for the rest, it was astonishing. Marie-Desneige had decoded the painting with such insight and lucidity that Ange-Aimée could also see the child in the orangey splotch, the mother's protective stance, and, on the side, in the yellow smudge, the father, also a protector, and on the father's lap, another child, in coral. He died crying, Marie-Desneige said.

'How do you do that?'

'I spent over sixty years deciphering everything that was said and not said around me. The gestures, the looks, everything they missed and that they thought went over my head, I understood; I stored it all up and at night, in my bed, I would play back the movie of my day, analyzing every scene, dissecting the slightest word, the smallest gesture. I looked back at everything. Survival in the asylum means that you always have to be on the lookout. It sharpens the senses.'

The photographer remembered what Bruno had said about his aunt. She sees things others don't.

'What else do you see?'

'That right now you want to take me to the other cabin. Your pores are dilated, you're warm, you're excited by the idea of the canvasses that are waiting in the other cabin.'

'There are hundreds of them.'

'Well, my poor dear, you'll have to wait because my bones are tired. Maybe tomorrow, if it's a nice day for a walk.'

Ange-Aimée had turned back into the photographer. All those canvasses piled up in their mystery, right there, close by, containing the story of a life, the story of a boy walking through smoking rubble, a man imprisoned by his ordeal –

the story that had escaped her during her research into the Great Fires was encoded in stains of colour that only Marie-Desneige had the key to.

But Marie-Desneige, at that moment, was very old. Pale, almost anemic, she was resting on Ted's chair, her back breaking with fatigue. The walk, on top of interpreting the paintings, had exhausted her. It was too much to ask, something that Ange-Aimée keenly regretted. Tomorrow, she decided, no walk. I'll come get the paintings and I'll bring them to her. Just a few, seven or eight, no more.

She was disappointed by how little commotion the news caused. The men had finished work at the plantation and were promising themselves a spot of fishing the next day as a reward for their labours. The trout from the lake's cool waters had more appeal than a riddle scribbled deep inside a painting. If Ted had wanted them to understand something, he would have done better than that, was Tom's only reaction. Bruno and Steve had smoked more than their fill; they were sluggish, buried under wide smiles, and the news only swallowed them up further. Nobody was surprised that a boy believed to be blind could eighty years later paint the scene that Marie-Desneige had shed light on. Only Charlie showed any surprise, but this was for Marie-Desneige, a long admiring look that no one missed.

So the next day was spent fishing. The trout were in a deep bay behind a point across the water from Ted's camp. It would take only twenty minutes by canoe to get there. The canoe was an old wooden craft. It could hold only four people at a time, so it took two trips to carry everyone to the other shore. The dogs followed swimming.

It was an enchanted spot. Hidden behind a narrow strip of land, the bay was home to a play of shadow and light on the lake's waters. On the shore there were a few rocky escarpments, interspersed with blond, sandy breaks, tiny beaches bathed in sunlight, and behind lush vegetation, a cedar forest with a smell of camphor that kept mosquitoes at bay. Therein lay the whole advantage of the spot.

They had a summer camp, a cabin in every way similar to the ones that served as their dwellings on the other shore. Furnished much more summarily, it had only a small, rudimentary stove, three bed frames piled with furs, a table, three chairs and, leaning against the wall, a counter and a few kitchen items. It was astonishing to think that three old men, almost a century old apiece and living in the middle of the forest, had felt the need for a place twenty minutes from their hideaway where they could get away during the sunny days of summer. *Like city folk with their cottages,* the photographer thought.

Ted was bound up in this place. He had been a silent companion but a devout fisherman, and the whole day, each time a trout nibbled, Ted came back to mind.

They talked a lot about Ted, how he cast his line, never a wasted movement, always in a patch of shade, and the beginnings of a smile when he got a bite, but never a word, not even when it was a nice catch; Ted's victories were private. Like the rest of it, he let nothing out, no shift in mood, no impatience; he remained silent on anything related to himself. And finally they talked, to the photographer's great satisfaction, about the paintings he had left behind that might contain parts of the answer to the mystery of Ted, but they were sceptical. No one had the answer, not even Ted, so why would he have gone to the trouble of explaining in paintings what wouldn't be understood?

Charlie disagreed. 'Ted probably had a life much fuller that anyone could have imagined. Of the three of us,' he said, 'he was the one who had the most to say, maybe too much, too much to be expressed in words. A man who spends the last twenty years of his life tearing out his hair to put meaning in stains of colour has a great deal to say.'

Charlie's words had a persuasive effect, and the next day, and those following, for the entire summer in fact, they tried to understand the mystery of Ted.

The paintings were brought to Marie-Desneige, five per day, no more, Charlie made sure of it, and carried back to their cabin, labelled and placed in chronological order. They told the story of the Great Matheson Fire, the photographer realized fairly quickly, as Ted had experienced it during his six days of wandering.

In total, three hundred and seventy-seven paintings that, for the most part, repeated the same motif, flashes of bright colour under a veil of smoke, but they found some in the lot that were luminous in the foreground. For example, paintings illustrating the initial moments after the fire. The photographer recognized them without Marie-Desneige having to decipher them, because of the golden light that survivors had talked to her about and that, on the canvas, consumed all the space, the charred tree trunks forming only a thin serrated line in the background. But it took Marie-Desneige's eye to detect the presence of bodies in the hazy black at the bottom of the painting.

Throughout the summer, the photographer put the pieces together, because Ted had not painted as one would write a novel, taking care to tell a story. He would be interested in a scene, and paint one or more versions of it, store them in the cabin and then launch into another scene, two days or five days later; the chronological order of his memories mattered very little to him. He painted to be free of them, to magnify them or to leave them to an improbable posterity. The thick layer of paint that covered the canvasses suggested that he had spent a lot of time on them.

Ted was not blind the whole time he wandered. The photographer doubted whether he had ever been, even partially. There were canvasses that illustrated episodes where the young Boychuck had been made out to be completely blind. The scene of the survivors in the pond, for instance – a completely surreal scene. Three men plunged waist-high in the muddy waters of a pond, a moose bathing in the same water, and a bird perched on the right shoulder of the youngest man. The photographer had a hard time recognizing the old man who had told her the story, the young man with the bird perched on his shoulder, but all the details were there, superimposed in thick flows of colour. It was impossible to escape this apocalyptic vision. He staggered through the rubble, the young old man had told her, as if he were walking in footsteps that were too big for him, as if he were walking in the footsteps of God.

Certain canvasses revealed episodes completely unfamiliar to her. No survivor had ever told her about the two young girls who had drifted down the Black River on a raft. Their hair, magnificently blond and luminous, covered their entire bodies. They were lying face down on the raft, and you could see only a trail of gold in what Marie-Desneige recognized as the black waters of a river. But she had been unable to interpret the trail of light in the black expanse. They needed other paintings that repeated the same motif from a different angle, and then still others where the young girls were standing or kneeling on the raft, for her to be able to make out human forms under the mass of hair. The same young girls appeared again in another series; Marie-Desneige recognized them immediately as they waved their arms above their head. *They cried and they pleaded – they had spotted someone on the opposite shore who could help them,* she said.

They appeared again a number of times over the summer. Charlie and Tom, who had been keeping their distance, started to take an interest in the young girls' story. Because it was just that, a story, which began when we saw them in the distance on the river, and then closer up, paddling with their hands, and then they were seen capsizing, or at least that's what Marie-Desneige presumed. This series was confused and hard to read, and the further they got into it, the less they understood. The paintings were nothing more than drips and splashes of vibrant colour. Ted had taken up spatula and drip painting.

The day came when Marie-Desneige, managing to read a particularly muddled painting, announced that it was a portrait of young girls. She showed them the lines to follow in the thick paste outlining the contour of the faces, the mouths, the cheeks, and where a flash of pink light bled through, the eyes and, what made the characters recognizable in the midst of it all, the golden filaments that intertwined them, their hair.

'The Polson twins!' Tom exclaimed, astonished at having recognized someone in all this chaos.

'Who?'

'The Polson twins were beauties, and their hair! Pure splendour! But Ted got it wrong. Their hair wasn't that long; it wasn't down to their ankles.'

Tom didn't know much about the two beauties. Born in Matheson to a Scottish father and a Latvian mother, they had become a town attraction. People came from as far away as Hearst to see them. Their beauty only grew, and in adolescence, the parents resolved to hide them from the eyes of the world. Too beautiful for such a small village. Tom didn't know anything about their odyssey on the Black River. He vaguely recalled that one of them married a man from Cochrane and the other set off on the road with a musician.

One thing was certain. They had made a big impression on the young Boychuck. There were thirty-two paintings devoted to them. Was Ted in love with one of them? Or both? It was a good question.

The day after the discovery of the portrait of the Polson twins, Charlie took Marie-Desneige to rest at the summer camp. It was the only way to put some distance between her and the paintings. The exercise was exhausting her.

The photographer took advantage of this day of rest to continue sorting and labelling the paintings. The most difficult part was giving each one a title. In the case of the series about the Polson twins, the titles were ready-made: *Young Girls With Long Hair 1, 2, 3,* up to *32*. But certain paintings remained untitled and waited along a wall of the cabin until the photographer had the right inspiration. There was *Child in the Stream* – that was what she called it in her mind, but she could not resign herself to giving it such a banal name. The drama that this child had lived through deserved more thought. There was also the entire series about the carnage in Nushka, apocalyptic images that could not find a voice. She had, however, isolated two paintings from the series, both *Crying Cow*. The title chose itself. The cow was literally in tears. In *Crying Cow 1,* the tears fell one by one like drops of rain on the devastated landscape, while they came in torrents in *Crying Cow 2.* She didn't understand why Ted indulged in such fantasy.

Marie-Desneige and Charlie returned at the end of the day, relaxed and smiling. The break had done them good.

They got back to reading paintings, but this time they were careful to give Marie-Desneige breaks. Deciphering the paintings was more demanding than it seemed, and after four or five days of work, Marie-Desneige would become flat and slow, with almost no visual acuity, *One day older*, she'd say with a weary smile, and Charlie would bring her to the summer camp.

In the North, summers are short and intense. A dry heat, with no breeze, still, that traps the air and leaves no other choice but to dive into the lake. And that's probably what Marie-Desneige and Charlie were doing. They came back from their breaks smiling more than ever, their hair dripping wet. Marie-Desneige as a prow head at the bow of the canoe, barely recognizable with her hair plastered to her head, and Charlie, in the back, paddling with a princely motion.

They were well into the summer when they came to the painting that would lend a whole other meaning to the photographer's quest. The painting was striking in its realism, completely different from the rest of Ted's oeuvre, a portrait that the photographer immediately identified. The woman painted in light tones on a purplish background had a gaze you could not take your eyes off. Enveloping, soft, almost caressing. This woman's presence was entirely in her eyes, either blue or green, it was hard to tell their colour, but the light that radiated from them left no doubt in the photographer's mind. The woman was younger by twenty or thirty years, she had less pronounced wrinkles, hair not yet completely grey, but the same pink light in the corner of her eyes. There was no doubt: it was the little old lady from High Park, the little old bird lady. One hundred and two years old, the photographer still wondered, was it possible?

On the painting, the sparkle of light was not mocking but loving.

'She's in love,' Marie-Desneige announced.

'In love?'

'With the person looking at her.'

They are at the summer camp, lying on a bed of furs, still dripping with water. They have just been swimming, and Marie-Desneige is exhausted from fighting off a panic attack. It came on without warning. They were swimming hand in hand, and Charlie felt Marie-Desneige's fingers tense slightly in his hand. They were up to their shoulders in the water when it happened.

Charlie immediately knew what was happening. She had a hard, concentrated look in her eyes.

He took her in his arms and brought her back to shore. She did not protest, did not move or say a word. She let herself be carried along, and once they reached the summer camp, when he wanted to lay her down on the furs, she stayed in his arms. She didn't want to let go of him. He held her close.

'There, it's over. It's passed.'

They are in the darkest corner of the cabin, but on this beautiful summer's day, even dark corners have some light, and Charlie follows the light that travels to every recess of Marie-Desneige's body.

They are naked.

The first few times, they swam in their underwear, but the discomfort of wet underwear once they were dressed convinced them to swim naked. Each reacted differently to the other's nakedness. Marie-Desneige stifled a giggle. Charlie's body, large up top, stood on little bow legs between which hung his genitals, which seemed to her enormous, disproportionate. As for Charlie, he could not take his eyes off the white bouquet of pubic hair. But they got used to seeing each other naked. Swimming was even more enjoyable with no clothes coming between the silky water and their skin.

'Shhhhh, no, please don't.'

She is so small in his arms, and he rocks her like a child.

'Shhhhhh, no, don't sing, please don't sing,' Charlie begs.

She is still struggling. She has not completely reassembled her body. Being rocked in Charlie's arms calms her a little, but brings back the plaintive song that helps her resurface. He can't handle the threnody. And to avoid hearing it, he starts to sing, one sound at a time, intoning three notes, a monotonous chant that comes to him from another life, when his wife was lulling the children to sleep.

'Lala-lala, lala-lala...'

The lullaby works. Marie-Desneige relaxes.

'There,' she says.

Charlie lays her on the furs and places his hand where she shows him to. The skin under his leathery palm is warm and soft.

'There,' she says again.

And the hand caresses her stomach under her sagging breast.

She smiles. She comes back to life. Charlie feels the knots of panic releasing under his hand.

'There?' he asks, indicating the white bouquet.

She smiles, naughty and flirtatious; she is thirty years younger. He has grown younger too. At that moment, they are fifty years old. Maybe twenty.

THE COLLECTION OF IMPOSSIBLE LOVES

'Miss Sullivan' was how the woman introduced herself the first time the photographer visited the small municipal museum of Matheson. No first name, only Miss, which she stressed like a noble title. The photographer remembered an old maid, withered, very tall, lanky and stooped. She could well have had flat feet and an inverted sacrum, the photographer thought, so out of balance did her bony, forbidding body seem. But so romantic it could bring tears to your eyes. To hear her tell it, the young Boychuck wandered days in the rubble looking for his beloved. That's what brought the photographer back to the little museum in Matheson.

She had brought Ted's portrait of the little old bird lady.

The lady at the museum had no trouble identifying her. Angie Polson, she said without hesitation. Angie was the one who took off with the musician. The other twin was Margie, and she died a long time ago. Angie was the more stunning of the two, the lady added. The photographer didn't doubt it.

She had also brought with her a few paintings from the *Young Girls With Long Hair* series. She held out no hope that the woman would be able to identify them. Even Marie-Desneige had a hard time deciphering the paintings. No, what she hoped was that she would tell her one more time about the flowers that had been spotted in the hands of the young wandering Boychuck. Flowers for his beloved, the woman had said. An old maid's romantic twaddle, the photographer had thought, but now she wondered whether this love story didn't have a kernel of truth.

When she announced her intention to go back to the museum in Matheson, Tom's response had been scathing. 'Tell me,' he said, 'are you this interested in other people's lives because you don't have one of your own?'

She was aware that her presence was the subject of comment and speculation at the hideaway. She was accepted and liked, they enjoyed her company, but they were worried that a woman, still young, in her early forties they figured, had no other needs. Of course, she went back to Toronto where she had matters to attend to, but as soon as those matters were settled, she came back to the hideaway. It was as if she knew no other way of living. In photos, in paintings and in life, she needed old people.

'You don't pay much attention to your life,' Charlie remarked one day.

'What about Bruno? And Steve?'

'That's different,' and he mimed smoking a joint.

There was no need to worry about Steve and Bruno, he said. They had a life all mapped out: marijuana and retiring in the middle of the forest. One day they would be the two old men at the hideaway, or they'd stay in the Lebanese man's hotel until the end of their days, if the hotel was still standing.

'Are you going to take care of them too when they're old?'

She didn't answer. Charlie was kidding himself if he thought he would have successors. Bruno had no calling to be a hermit in the forest. And Steve – well, Steve, yes, maybe, you couldn't really tell with Steve. He truly didn't care what the future held. As for her, she had no particular penchant for pot, a little bit here and there, nothing more, and no calling to be a caregiver. She had slipped into the role of Ange-Aimée out of compassion, out of friendship, and then in the end she found it suited her, this skin that was not hers and that was comforting, consoling and supportive. But since they had discovered the paintings, she had found her old personality, and that was what sent her back to the museum in Matheson.

Miss Sullivan was delighted. Visitors were rare, return visitors even rarer, and there was a magnificent love story in the bundle of paintings her guest had brought with her. Magnificent, painful, secret: the perfect ingredients.

She hadn't known the Polson twins when their beauty was in full bloom. 'I'm too young,' she said, 'sixty-six years old.' The photographer found her desire to reveal her age charming. She offered the hoped-for reaction.

'You don't look it.'

She did look it, easily, but sixty-six was indeed too young to have known the Polson twins when they were the wonders of Matheson. She had known them later. Miss Sullivan was then fifteen, was called Virginia, was already tall and thin and very romantic, and had been waiting for her mother to finish chatting with the owner of the general store, where they had gone for grommets for their drapes, when they saw Angie Polson pass by the window at a brisk pace heading toward the train station.

'There goes a girl who's not afraid to be a bother,' her mother or the clerk had said.

Angie Polson was nothing like the other women in Matheson. That was her unforgivable sin. Elegant, poised and stylish, she was suspected of having a secret life in Toronto or somewhere else, since, at over forty, she was unmarried and childless, and still just as beautiful. An original, from the big Bohemian scarf to the vertiginously high heels. No one in Matheson dressed like that, or had that energy, that freedom. The young Virginia was filled with admiration.

At the age of fifteen, she already looked like the old maid she would become, but that same little heart beat in the same chest, and this rebellious woman filled with ardent, tumultuous love, probably forbidden love, whom she had seen pass in front of the general store, became the emblem of the life she would never have. She knew that the great love she dreamed of simply would not be.

Who had Angie Polson been bothering? Everyone and no one in particular – her mother's remark or the clerk's came from that inexhaustible supply of nasty comments that small towns keep circulating day in and day out.

And so the tall, thin and romantic Virginia Sullivan started to collect the scattered fragments of the secret loves of Angie Polson, which made her particularly sensitive to anything that was said or sighed in Matheson. She found out more than she need to know about people's lives. Jealousies, grudges, vengeance, horrible secrets and small redemptions, she herself was astonished with what she collected. Listening to the slightest peep that reached her ears, piecing together and pulling apart everything she had been told, she became highly skilled in the art of the secret. This was how she guessed the secret loves of just about everyone in Matheson.

The photographer didn't understand what she meant when the long grey silhouette bent over her and asked, in a conspiratorial tone, 'Do you want to see my collection?'

From the wide smile that met her astonished eyes, she understood that she was having bestowed upon her a great honour.

'There is nothing more beautiful than an impossible love.'

The notebook that Miss Sullivan placed in her hands was as plain as plain can be. A cardboard cover, spiral bound, lined paper. On the front were two monograms joined by a heart. While the monograms were elaborate and highly stylized, the heart was of a heartrending naiveté. Red, obviously, and pierced by Cupid's arrow, it trickled a few drops of blood like an icon of Christ. Clearly the old maid liked hearts that bled. And there were many of them, bleeding hearts, in the glass armoire from which she pulled this notebook, and then another and another. She had twenty in all.

'My collection,' she said in a slow, soft voice.

In love, thought the photographer, it was the voice of a woman in love. Can a woman truly find satisfaction in the loves of strangers that were never even fulfilled?

The notebooks told stories that were profoundly sad, love burning in the hearts, but rarely in the joining of bodies, and yet these tales had a certain grace, a certain redemption. The adoring gaze of the old maid. No matter whether the bodies had come together, the important thing was the step by timid, awkward step of two beings drawn toward one another that an anonymous observer followed devotedly, noting the day and time when the man had said hello to the woman, her gesture to distance herself from the arm of her husband, and the weather the next day when the woman came back alone, at the same time, to the same place, searching for the one who was watching her from a place he could not leave. They could carry on this way for years in a delicious two-step, neither ever crossing the forbidden line. The observer's attention never wavered. She noted everything. The changes in hairstyle, the appearance of cleavage, a starched collar, closer contact, light touches and soft looks, but once the possibility of crossing over the forbidden line appeared, it was pure elation, the observer could no longer contain herself. Would he or wouldn't he answer the letter? If he wrote her a letter in turn, would there be a moonlit rendezvous, passionate kisses, an exchange of promises, more rendezvous, more kisses, and the husband, wild with rage, pique and pain, what would he do? She wrote about it for pages and pages, and the photographer read this, clearly seeing that the old maid's concern was that if this love came to be, it would belong to her no more.

At the end of notebook; *GR bleeding heart YT*, because rather than face a jealous husband, GR contented herself with a single passionate rendezvous.

One notebook particularly intrigued the photographer. The bleeding heart was there, preceded by the monogram *JM*, but in place of the second monogram, there was a question mark.

'I never found out who she loved,' Miss Sullivan explained. 'She was in love, of that I am sure. There was an absence in her that cannot be mistaken, an air of never actually being where she was. I searched around her, looking for the man who inhabited her. For years I followed her, to the train station, the post office, everywhere. I was hoping for a letter, a mysterious traveller, but nothing. She died with her secret and an air of waiting for someone who did not come, not even to her funeral. I was there, and the only man I saw weeping was her father. She died at thirty from having cried too much. Pleurisy, they said. It's an apt word. The word *pleurisy* contains the word *pleur*, French for *cry*, and not even the slightest hint of suicide. It's the saddest story in my collection.'

On the cover of the last notebook were three monograms, *AP*, *MP* and *TB*, around a heart pierced with two arrows.

'He loved them both.'

So this was the story of the Polson twins and Boychuck compiled in a compact script by Miss Sullivan from the moment when, as young Virginia, she had spotted Angie Polson through the general store window. The final entry in the notebook was dated just a year earlier, when the photographer came to her museum looking for information about the survivors of the Great Fires and more particularly about Boychuck. *Did this woman have a message for Theodore?*, the old maid asked in the notebook. *Had Angie entrusted this woman with a message?*

The photographer flipped through the notebook, gleaning a few sentences here and there, enough to understand that the story was hopeless. All three of them orbited around this love that kept them at a distance yet bound in a magnetic sphere that had complete power over them. There was much to-ing and fro-ing, many depressing setbacks, nobody was ever in the right place at the right time. The young Virginia followed them until she became an old maid. And always the same question returned in her sharp, tightly packed script: *would Theodore end up choosing?*

'Theodore?'

The photographer was intrigued. Where did this new first name come from?

Theodore Boychuck was what was written on the envelopes. *Theodore Boychuck, General Delivery, Matheson, Ontario.* Sometimes in long, fine letters, sometimes in childlike loops. The twins did not share temperament or handwriting.

'Theodore was his real first name.'

The letters they sent him via General Delivery were the tenuous thread that held the whole story together. The young Virginia didn't miss a single letter. Every day, under the pretext of going to get her parents' mail, she went to the post office, and because she was an avid reader, and therefore literate, which was not the case for many people in Matheson, she was asked to read letters and sometimes to write them. The post mistress, not very educated herself, got into the habit of turning to her for official correspondence. One thing led to another, and she ended up helping sort the mail as well, which led to her discovery of this strange three-way dance foreshadowed each time by two letters sent to General Delivery.

She recorded in her notebook the date and place of the postmark of both letters, normally a few days apart, since one came from Toronto and the other from Cochrane, and the date of the arrival at the train station of a man that she easily recognized. The man, tall and sombre, headed to a rooming house, left his luggage there, and then went to the post office to pick up the two letters that were waiting for him. Everything was noted in detail: his clothes, his pace, the amount of time spent at the rooming house, the way he had of nodding his head to offer thanks when handed the letters, but not a word. The still-young old maid had never heard him utter a single word.

Obviously she read the letters. How could she have followed the whole story if she had not been a witness? She spirited them away from the post mistress, steamed them open, read them, copied long excerpts in her notebook and brought them back intact, ready to be delivered to their addressee.

Dear Fedor, they began, or *Dear Fedia*. An affectionate diminutive of Theodore, the old maid explained. Angie was more comfortable using *Dear Fedia*, while Margie generally stuck to *Dear Fedor*, although the salutation could change from one to the other.

'They both loved him.'

The letters that arrived in Matheson did not arrange rendezvous but made references to rendezvous elsewhere, to other letters he or she had written or had or had not received, to changes of address, particularly in the case of

Theodore, who, it seemed, had no fixed address, moving from place to place as work became available, which required the two women to follow a veritable maze of general deliveries along the railways that served Ontario, which they sometimes complained about in their letters. *When will you settle down somewhere?*

The letters attested to heartbreaking advances and setbacks. Sometimes it was Angie who wrote that dear Fedia should understand that her sister Margie would not survive without his love; sometimes it was Margie who stepped aside and asked her dear Fedor to forget her, because she was now married to a man who cherished her, and to go to her sister who was free and had waited for him for so many years. Since Theodore could not choose, the sisters decided to do it in his stead. This incredible sacrifice that each was prepared to make was all for naught, since Theodore, unable to make a decision, simply obeyed and went from one to the other without any of them finding happiness.

The letters referred to a whole history of missed rendezvous, failures and misunderstandings, the most difficult period being the six years during which they had no news from their dear Theodore. He had left Matheson, intending never to return, because he believed them drowned in the Black River. They in turn thought he was in Toronto. This period was decisive. The first missteps forever sealed how they would live this three-way love. The letters often referred to it: *how could we have gotten lost along so many parallel roads?*

At age eighteen, Angie ran away to Toronto with a musician who was passing through, in the hopes of finding Theodore there. But Theodore was over a thousand kilometres to the west, a longshoreman in Port Arthur. Two years later, he decided to face his ghosts and got off the train at

Matheson. But Margie was in Cochrane, married to a hardware store owner, and Angie was waiting for him in Toronto.

'Angie was single. He could have married her, couldn't he?' the photographer said, exasperated.

'Yes, he could have, but he loved Margie too.'

'So why did Margie marry the man in Cochrane?'

'To step aside for Angie.'

'Good lord!'

The story was beginning to twist and turn a bit too much for the photographer's taste, but clearly all of these amorous complications thrilled Miss Sullivan. Her cheeks had coloured slightly, and her eyes were shining like marbles in the sun.

But the story had the merit of answering the question about the Great Matheson Fire. What had kept young Boychuck wandering for six days? *Love, there is only love,* the photographer thought, *to explain what we don't understand.* She was still struggling with Boychuck's new first name, but she imagined a young Theodore in love in the smoking rubble, going back and forth along the shore of the Black River searching for two young girls. The paintings in the series *Young Girls With Long Hair* took on meaning, particularly the one in which Marie-Desneige was able to identify a raft capsizing in the churning black water. Young Theodore had witnessed the scene. He couldn't rescue them, and he had wandered for days hoping to find them.

It was more than she had hoped for from her meeting with the lady at the museum. She had come merely to confirm her intuition, and she left with a story that reconstructed the identity of the very old woman who had started her on this quest.

The little old lady of High Park was one of the two young girls with long hair. Miss Sullivan had clearly identified her.

First, on the painting that depicted her at sixty-something, and then on the one where she was shown with her twin sister.

'One hundred and two? She would be one hundred and two years old. Is that possible?' the photographer wondered.

The smile of a person who isn't in the habit of smiling is a thing of rare beauty; it lights up her entire face. Miss Sullivan's smile was a radiant sun.

'Angie was always mischievous,' she replied. 'She likes a bit of fun.'

Miss Sullivan was thrilled to know that Angie Polson was alive. She hadn't had any news for such a long time. No appearance by the former marvel of Matheson, no letter sent General Delivery for Theodore Boychuck for over twenty years.

She was not surprised to learn of Boychuck's death.

'He trailed death behind him.'

Theodore Boychuck's death, however, meant the end of her collection. The *AP MP TB* notebook was her last active file. She was expecting no more.

'Ill-fated love is impossible these days.'

The photographer felt relieved as she left her. The life of this woman who had never found, or even searched for, what she needed was tragic.

They are feeling sluggish. Time stretches out each gesture, each thought. Charlie is lying on his left side above Marie-Desneige, who receives his caresses. Charlie's hands are soft and penetrating. They explore her knees, her ankles, missing nothing. They come and go on her thighs, inside her thighs, slowly, methodically, they caress, palpate, knead, and when they reach the crease of her bottom, the pubic bouquet, the hands slowly drift off course.

He leans over her. His great tousled white head starts to sniff her entire body. 'You smell like vanilla,' he tells her when he gets tangled in her hair. He nestles in her neck, moves down her shoulders, takes a long draw of her armpits. 'You smell like spring,' he says, and she smiles. 'And you don't smell like winter anymore,' she tells him in turn, and they both smile at the thought of the strong odour of wool underwear that permeates their winter bed.

Charlie's great head moves down along her chest, burrows in the hollow of her breasts, two little empty wineskins that he caresses with his fingertips and then more boldly, more generously, while he moves further down still, breathing in deeply, exploring, leaving his hot breath along her skin as he travels. Marie-Desneige lets him breathe her in like a flower to be picked, water to be drunk. She lets Charlie's hot breath envelope her, penetrate her.

He is at her stomach. Soft, tender and with the scent of cinnamon, he says, when after stopping at the navel and its odour of deep earth, he discovers the purplish scar under the fold of skin at the spot that hides an old wound. The scar is long, horizontal and hard to the touch. He raises his eyes to Marie-Desneige.

'It's from the baby,' she says.

He blows on the scar, he caresses it, kisses it, and then

refolds the skin over the wound. Nothing shows, the past can be left alone.

He slowly lets himself slide where Marie-Desneige waits for him and breathes in the odour of land and sea, he smoothes her hair with his tender fingers, he covers it with his hot breath and then he raises his head and sees Marie-Desneige smiling at him and calling him, and he comes back to the smell of her hair, spread out alongside her.

Thus begins the slow work of bodies coming together, which in their case is difficult, because they have neither the youth nor the training required. But slowly they find their rhythm. Legs interlace, tongues entwine, bodies embrace, rock each other under the layer of fur. But age soon rears its head, breathing becomes laboured, and in Charlie's case comes out in coughs, and the bodies have to separate, abandon one another, side by side, defeated by the effort.

They do not actually consummate their relationship, never will; it has been too long for both of them.

'You had a child?'

Charlie's voice is hesitant. He wants to comfort, console, bandage wounds, but in his voice there is his own wound, that of a man emasculated by old age.

'A long time ago.'

'Was it a girl or a boy?'

'I don't know. They didn't tell me.'

'Did you have other children?'

'No, I suppose that they did a hysterectomy while they were doing the Caesarean.'

Marie-Desneige snuggles up to him, very feminine, worried about what he is thinking.

'Thank you,' she says, knowing that he will ask what for.

But he doesn't ask.

She explains that she has never experienced this, kisses, embraces. She has only ever known business hastily done in a stairwell, behind a hedge, skirt hiked up, and a man in a hurry to get on with it and finish, sometimes a resident, sometimes an attendant, as young or as old as she, but she didn't complain. She always liked bidiwiwi.

'Bidiwiwi?'

'We didn't have another word for it.'

'And you liked ... bidiwiwi?'

'A lot. Even when I was forced, I managed to get pleasure from it. But I've never been kissed, never caressed.'

'This is your first kiss?'

'My first kiss and it's much better than anything I could have imagined.'

'You will have all the kisses you like, I promise you. All the kisses you never had, millions of kisses, billions and trillions of caresses.'

'We'll have to live a very long time for that.'

'So what's stopping us?'

'Promise me that as long as I'm alive, you will never touch your box of salt.'

'I promise.'

'Promise me that as long as you're alive, you will never let me go near your box of salt.'

'I promise.'

'Even at the peak of a crisis, even when I beg you, promise me.'

'I promise.'

A WOLF IN THE NIGHT

'No, that man couldn't love.'

The photographer had returned to the hideaway with this crazy love story, wondering who would react most strongly. *They won't want to believe it,* she told herself. And yet the one person who should have been touched by the romance of the story was rejecting the very idea of Ted being in love.

Marie-Desneige was decided. *A man who has images of such horror within him, who is fuelled by them to the point of obsession, is incapable of love. When suffering takes hold of someone, it leaves no room for anything else. I have seen men and women suffer to the point of loving their pain, stoking it, adding new torments to it. I have seen them mutilate themselves, heap abuse upon themselves, roll around in their feces, and I'm not even talking about suicide attempts. An attempt is suffering; suicide is the decision to put an end to it. And there were plenty of attempts. Suicides too.*

She had never said so much. They listened to her attentively. They were on what they called Marie-Desneige's veranda, the space at the front of the house they had thought of screening in but never had, though the idea remained, and they talked quietly on that mild evening at the end of the summer, each sitting on a stump, paying no attention to the buzzing of mosquitoes, as if they were truly protected by screens on Marie-Desneige's veranda.

The air was filled with the smell of earth and grass that has been scorched all summer by the sun. A light breeze had come up. The evening was mild, cocoon-like, perfect for conversation.

The photographer had arrived at the end of the afternoon with a restaurant meal for everyone. Fries, salad, roast chicken and a love story that, now that Marie-Desneige had declared Ted incapable of love, went off in every which way. No one understood anything, but they accepted Marie-Desneige's opinion. She had access to a part of Ted that remained off limits to them in spite of their years of companionship. His paintings, it seemed, contained more than anything he could have told them, more than he knew about what drove, obsessed and tormented him.

'Too many deaths,' she explained. 'Too many bodies, too much black coiled at the bottom of his paintings, never any light, or, if there is any, it's to illuminate blackened bodies, cries of horror, hands outstretched where death surprised them. No one can live with that deep within. Ted tried to free himself from it, to hurl all of that horror onto the canvas. Maybe he succeeded in a sense. His final painting, the one on his easel, had light – very little, a faint glimmer, but enough to create a space from which he could slip away gently. That's what I hope for him, it's what I hope for all of us. To slip away gently.'

On that, their old friend, feeling their call, rose from a secret place and went to meet their thoughts. Death is never very far from the elderly.

To die at ninety-four isn't so bad. Ted may not have been the happiest of men, but he had held his own, and he died free, with dignity, not even needing help when his hour came. Charlie respected that. Leaving without insisting on goodbyes is a sign of respect for those you leave behind. Goodbyes do no one any good. And then he thought of Marie-Desneige. If one of them were to die – and it would happen, it had to happen one day – on that day, would he be willing to part without a goodbye? The thought muddled his mind.

Tom was also tangled up in his thoughts. It was the end of August. Fall was coming soon and then winter, and he was wondering whether it wouldn't be better to end things there, in the balmy warmth of the end of summer. He remembered the previous winter with bitterness, the flu that had kept him in bed for weeks, spoon-fed bouillon by the photographer, as helpless as a newborn. The flu had left him weakened, with lungs that did not inhale in unison and the feeling that his body did not want to follow him.

Death had no hold on Steve or Bruno, but they felt her prowling around Tom and Charlie.

'If the little old lady in High Park is really one of the Polson twins, what are you going to do for your exhibition?' Steve asked to lighten the mood.

'I don't know yet,' the photographer answered.

They knew about the project. She had talked to them about it before visiting the lady at the museum. The idea had slowly developed as the paintings were deciphered, and she realized that a number of them had echoes in the photos in her portfolio. That was how, from one painting to the next, from one story to the next, she arrived at the idea of a dual exhibition, with Boychuck's paintings and her photos of the survivors.

In some cases, she could even imagine the copy on the card accompanying certain pairs, the card for *Castaways of the Pond*, for example – that was what she had called the painting of the three men who had taken refuge in a pond, with an enormous silhouette of a moose behind them and a bird perched on the shoulder of the youngest man, Joseph

Earle, the one who had told her the story and of whom she had a picture. It was a working title. She had also considered *The Last Humans on Earth* to express the feeling that inhabited the three men in the pond or, more explicitly, *Waiting for the End of the World.*

The text should first describe the scene, because Ted had painted a black maelstrom surrounded by a ring of diffuse light, which murky forms emerged from. The photographer had not yet decided what would come next in the text; it was heading off in too many directions at once. The light was what she wanted to explain first: the golden light after the apocalypse, the hand of God held out to these men in the pond that they were reluctant to take, not knowing whether they were still alive or already in the other world, and the boy with the vacant gaze whom they had seen pass. She didn't know if she should mention him in the text too.

The text that would introduce the photo of Joseph Earle was, however, very clear in her mind.

> Joseph Earle, January 1995. Born in Matheson in 1900. Arriving in Ramore at age ten, he worked on the family farm, held different jobs before becoming a gardener for Ontario Northland Railways, a job he held until his retirement. He now lives in the Croatian quarter of Timmins, formerly Schumacher. He was sixteen years old at the time of the Great Matheson Fire. Shown at the far right in the painting, he is with his cousins, Donald and Patrick McField.

Joseph and his cousins were surprised by the fire as they returned from the family still. The three young men had spent the night making alcohol that they sold to a bootlegger in Matheson. Moonshine, the old Joseph had said, proud of this fact, as if to say, *I didn't spend my whole life soaking in holy water*. It was an amusing anecdote, and the photographer could have used it in her accompanying text if she hadn't been worried about heading down paths that would take her farther from what she was trying to say. She wanted simple text. Her thinking wasn't yet very far along, but she knew that the emotion the paintings exuded would be amplified by the testimony of the photo and that nothing should get in the way of the synergy between the painting and the photo. So not too much chattering on the cards.

But anecdote sometimes gets at the essence of things, and she knew that she could not avoid the story told by a pair she had entitled *The Miracle of a Birth,* once again a working title, because the old man in the photo had yet to be born when he was depicted in the painting – he was still in his mother's womb, which was buried under two feet of earth. The scene in and of itself was not terribly disturbing: you could see only black mixed with long brown smears under a sky compressed by thick drips of grey. The interest of the painting lay in a light stroke of the brush from which emerged a point of light in the black impasto, the air hole through which the mother of the child to be born breathed. The text would have to explain this; otherwise it would be impossible to understand. The couple chased by the flames, Black River as their obstacle, neither of them knowing how to swim, a shovel abandoned on the shore, they dug a hole for shelter, a violent gust of wind, the flames rushed toward them, the man having just enough time to cover his wife with earth and to jump in the river clinging to a willow branch.

The branch broke, and I found myself without a father. It was young Boychuck who got us out of there. Seventy-nine years later, the miracle child inside him still marvelled at having had a life to live. His name was Thomas Verner; he had large doe-like eyes and a permanent smile.

Thomas Verner, May 1995. Born in Matheson in 1916. He spent his whole life on a farm, first in Charlton on the farm of the uncle who took him and his mother in after the Great Matheson Fire, and then in Belle Vallée, where he raised five children. He lives there to this day.

He lives there to this day. The photographer wondered whether she should go back to Belle Vallée to be sure. The photo was taken two years earlier. The old man with the angelic smile trailed an oxygen tank behind him and breathed though a nasal tube that he did not tolerate well. He removed it all the time and put it back just as fast, when his lungs whistled impatiently.

Thomas Verner was the youngest of her collection of old folks. A number were in danger of breathing their last breaths before the exhibition. 'Tell me you're not going to make the rounds of all your old fogies to find out if they're still sucking air,' Charlie objected. 'Are you this interested in the lives of others because you don't have one of your own?'

She thought then of the old maid at the museum who collected impossible loves just as she collected old miracle survivors. Was her own life tragic as well?

Tom and Charlie weren't thrilled about her plans for an exhibition.

Bruno and Steve were more co-operative. They had helped her organize and label the paintings, packing the ones she had taken to the Matheson museum and the ones for the exhibition, over one hundred of them, grouped in series, well identified and numbered, all were waiting in Ted's cabin to be loaded into the pickup to be transported to Toronto.

Something lingered in the air of this waning summer evening, something that reached them without them realizing it. The mildness of this late evening demanded that they turn their minds to time gone by, that they linger over it, that they consider it carefully before letting it go.

That's what they did, each in their own way, without realizing it.

One year had gone by since Marie-Desneige and the photographer had suddenly appeared in their lives. One year and one month, Charlie counted, still amazed at what had happened to him. *An old man in love, that's what I've become,* and he felt buoyant thinking about Marie-Desneige's little laugh in the furs. *How much more time will we have?*

Marie-Desneige was sitting at his side, as she always was. Everywhere they went, fishing, in the forest, picking berries, they were always together. The hours, the days, the months, the weeks – she lived them in detached moments, one by one, without considering the passage of time. How many more days, how many more months? The question did not have to be asked as long as there was this man whose broad hand kept her here on earth. It was his strength, his weight, his gravity, his earthly attraction.

Tom looked at the couple they formed, sitting beside one another, calm and peaceful in the falling night. How had they arrived there? The loves he had known had been like lightning bolts, meteoric, scorching. He had never given them the time to get to this state of completeness, jostled about as he was by life. How had they managed it? He was curious, not envious or bitter. He could have been – he had lost a lot in this affair – but he was not a man to brood. He had learned that you have to adjust how you row when the wind changes direction, and he quickly developed other habits now that they had formed a sort of community with these two women who just happened their way. Not envious or bitter, but curious. He wanted to put his finger on the thing that had always escaped him.

It was time for taking stock and reflecting. The evening was quickly turning to black night. The air was growing thicker with each person's reflections, and nobody wanted to pull away from this warm intimacy.

The photographer was still trying to answer Steve's question. What was she going to do if she couldn't find Angie Polson again?

I should have taken her picture when I had the chance, she admonished herself. She remembered the sparkle of pink light, her desire to capture that light, and then the conversation that followed, the Matheson Fire, the birds dropping out of the sky like flies – and then it was too late. The old lady had left, taking her one hundred and two years and her mischievous smile with her.

She needed a picture of Angie Polson to accompany the series *Young Girls with Long Hair.*

She had hoped that the lady at the museum would tell her how to find her, but the old maid had not seen her for over twenty years. The last time was in November 1972 at her mother's funeral. Miss Sullivan remembered it well. Everybody in Matheson remembered old Mrs. Polson's funeral and her daughter Angie arriving in a Cadillac with an elegant younger man. No one ever found out whether he was her husband, her son or her chauffeur, because she had not introduced him to anyone, and he stayed in the background during the service. More elegant and more capricious than ever, Angie wore a black silk dress that absorbed all the light and all the attention. Too beautiful for her age, that's what was said afterward in Matheson. At seventy years old, you don't walk about in a dress that dances on your legs, with a man who could be your lover.

Miss Sullivan recorded the fact in her notebook. Shortly afterward, she heard a rumour that Ted Boychuck had retreated into the forest. She recorded the rumour. But she had nothing else to offer. Nothing about the identity of the man at the funeral, nothing that could have led the photographer to Angie Polson's door to ask her to pose.

That's where she was in her thinking. Night had fallen, a black velvet humming in every direction, and in this muffled softness, her endeavour seemed to be cumbersome and complicated. Going from gallery to gallery, explaining the concept, convincing them, and everything that would follow, negotiating a contract, the opening, not to mention Angie Polson, whom she had not given up on finding – it all seemed very far away from the person who was enjoying the fresh air in the forest in the company of her friends, hermits of these woods.

She was leaving the next day with her cargo of paintings. Bruno would transport the remaining paintings in his truck. He had volunteered his help. Steve would never have made such an offer. In all his years managing a ghost hotel, he had never left his realm except for the two hundred kilometres to and from the next town.

So all of Ted's paintings found themselves in a warehouse in Toronto. Not a single one was left at the hideaway. It was an easy decision to make. They all agreed that the paintings would be much better off in a warehouse, dry and safe, than in Ted's cabin.

It was probably the idea of seeing the paintings leave the next morning that made the night so nostalgic and them so aware of the passage of time. Once the paintings were gone, it was as if nothing would remain of Ted, nothing of the summer they had spent together trying to understand what Ted had been trying to say in the canvasses.

A wolf howled in the night, and their attention focused on its call, coming to them from far off in the hills. The howl of the wolf can't help but move you. Even the most hardened of hearts, those who have heard it night after night for years, feel its pull. The fear of the wolf is an ancient one. The powers of the forest awaken in the night, and the insignificance of your humanity curls into a tight fist in the pit of your stomach.

The dogs started to howl in turn.

'It won't last long,' Tom said, 'just long enough for them to acknowledge each other's territory.'

The comment was meant to comfort Marie-Desneige. The wolves terrified her. A year spent in the forest had managed to calm many of her fears, but not that one. When a wolf howled, and they were gathered around a fire, they forgot about the ball knotted in their stomachs and turned toward Marie-Desneige.

Tom could see nothing. The night was too deep, but he could feel the sharp points of fear take hold of Marie-Desneige. Beside her, Charlie said not a word, made no move, but his constant attention, all of his being, was absorbed by Marie-Desneige and her fight against panic and terror.

And in the dark of the night, something happened that did not escape Tom's attention. Charlie's hand left his thigh and went to lie on Marie-Desneige's thigh, where her hand was clenched in a tight fist, which Charlie unfolded and brought back to his own thigh, a gesture that Tom followed in the dark and that moved him deeply. The two hands interlaced on Charlie's thigh was the image of a happiness he had never known. A couple, a real couple, united in a moment that belonged to them alone and that was enough for them.

The howling stopped, the dogs went back to sleep, the night was exuding comfort, and Tom wanted to know: 'Tell me, Marie-Desneige, are you completely happy?'

It was a strange question, and it took everyone by surprise. Marie-Desneige's answer, after a moment of hesitation, was an even greater surprise.

'I have everything I need. I could never have hoped for more, but I wouldn't mind seeing a car go by from time to time.'

And she explained that her greatest pleasure in that other life to which she would never ever return was that moment during the day or the evening, no matter, when she sat in front of the window and watched cars go by.

'Watching cars go by is very pleasant. There's always movement, it never stops. It empties your mind, and without you realizing it, you're somewhere else. It's very pleasant.'

Marie-Desneige behind a window in the asylum or on the steps in a Toronto suburb, letting herself be lulled by a parade of cars until she was somewhere else may have been a pleasant image for everyone on the veranda, but not for Charlie, who had just discovered that Marie-Desneige's happiness in the forest was not complete.

They paddled in silence, Tom in the front, Charlie in the back, Marie-Desneige in the middle with the dogs swimming behind them.

They have been there for a day and a night and they are waiting.

They are waiting for things to settle down on the other side of the bay.

No panic, no alarm, they are safe. They just have to wait.

The day had started like any other. A reticent sun, a jay that came to greet them, a hare speeding by: fall was in fine form.

They ate a breakfast of corned beef and peaches in syrup. No tea. They didn't want to light the stove. The smoke would give them away.

They are in front of the summer camp listening for noises coming from the hideaway.

It's dead calm. All that can be heard is the gentle wind in the cedars and the lapping of the water.

'I think it's over.'

'Yep, they're gone.'

'That's something to celebrate.'

Tom pulls a bottle out from his bag. Scotch. A bottle he had with him when he arrived at the hideaway and that he always refused to open out of fear that the desire to keep going would send him back to cavernous hotels and a social worker.

He lifts the bottle to gaze at the amber liquid in the sun, but the bottle is too dirty to let light through.

'Cheers!'

He pours himself a glass, offers one to Charlie and to Marie-Desneige, who decline, and knocks it back in one shot.

'I've never forgotten the taste.'

He pours another glass that he holds on to and swirls to watch the liquid turn in the hollow of his hand. The pleasure is intense. He closes his eyes to savour it.

'It's as good as it used to be. All that's missing is the clinking of ice cubes.'

Marie-Desneige searches at her feet and finds three round pebbles that she places in Tom's glass.

This time, he savours small swigs, making the ice cubes tinkle, attentive to his pleasure. He lets the amber liquid do its work.

At the third glass, he has reached a state of slowness that satisfies him. Slowly, very slowly, he gets up and, using the shovel that awaits him against the wall of the cabin, he lifts a first scoop of earth.

TWO GRAVES

The photographer had scoured Queen Street for three weeks for a gallery owner willing to show Ted's paintings. But each gallery had its specialty, and none fit with Ted's work, so she returned to the hideaway with a bitter sense of failure.

She knew immediately that something had happened. No quad in front of the hotel, no Steve or Darling to greet her, and in front of the main door left wide open, deep grooves in the earth, an army of vehicles that had left their tracks. She hurried to the great hall and what she saw confirmed what she already knew. The police had been there. Furniture overturned and torn open, strips of floorboards torn up – they hadn't exactly been wearing kid gloves. Even the Lebanese owner's animal collection had been taken down from the walls.

The scenario of a police raid had been studied time and time again. The photographer was familiar with all the details. Steve could recognize a member of the narcotics squad at a glance, and if one ever showed his face at the hotel, he would send Darling to warn Charlie. It had never happened, but they had planned for it.

So she went to Charlie's camp – empty, just as she expected. Marie-Desneige's house as well. On the shore of Ted's camp, she breathed a sigh of relief. The canoe was gone. They had hidden out at the summer camp. They had followed the plan to the letter.

She was relieved, but perplexed. What should she do now?

She went to Tom's and then to the plantation. Everything had been ripped up; there was nothing left. Thousands of beautiful mature marijuana plants vanished into an unholy mess. Here again, they hadn't pulled any punches. She thought of Steve, no doubt in jail by now, and Bruno, who, if he had had the good luck not to be there when the raid went down, would not be back anytime soon. Would she ever see them again? She felt cheated, abandoned by friendships that couldn't even be bothered to exchange addresses. Bruno who? Steve who? She didn't know their full names. *What if,* she thought, *it's Marc and Daniel, not Bruno and Steve, and I got to know them under false names?* The reality had an oppressive fuzziness to it. She felt as though she were walking through the smoke and gas of a disaster, the meaning of which escaped her.

Once again she found herself in front of Ted's camp. The lake was calm, windless; not a ripple disturbed the stillness. She stayed on the shore a long time searching the point of land behind which lay her friends' bay.

She would have to cross the lake. It was obvious, but impossible without a canoe.

So she got to work. She went from cabin to cabin, found tools, beams, bits of board and plywood and set about building a raft. Not very long, not very wide, just enough to hold her weight during the crossing.

She wondered what state she would find them in, Marie-Desneige in particular, so fragile and so powerless. The summer camp did not have all the comforts of her little house. Had she brought the things she needed? The nights were starting to get cold. Did she have time to grab warm clothes in the rush to get away?

She left her work and went to Marie-Desneige's house. The disorder didn't upset her; she had already seen it all. What interested her were the clothes thrown in a pile on the floor. She knew Marie-Desneige's entire wardrobe. She looked for what was missing.

What was missing were her black pants, her orange sweatshirt and her plaid shirt – no doubt what she was wearing at the time, which reassured the photographer, because the plaid shirt was incredibly warm. But what really surprised her, because you wouldn't expect an old woman who has just found out that she has to make a run for it to take such a useless item of clothing with her, was that her nightgown was missing. But then maybe it wasn't surprising, the nightgown being the most feminine and precious thing in Marie-Desneige's wardrobe.

Something else was missing that did not immediately attract her attention. She was searching through the mess in the house looking for Marie-Desneige's winter parka, when she felt something brush up against her leg. *Monseigneur,* she thought. It was only a dish towel that had fallen limply at her feet, but the sensation of the fabric against her leg reminded her that she hadn't seen or heard Marie-Desneige's cat since arriving at the hideaway.

She found the parka under the bed but not the cat. She went to Charlie's, still no cat – it wasn't until she was closing the door to Charlie's cabin that an image emerged — very clear, impossible to dispel — and forced her to backtrack. The image had burned itself into her brain and showed what, in her haste or in the depths of her unconscious, she hadn't registered or wanted to see. She returned to the cabin, already knowing what awaited her, and forced herself to look. There was no tinplate box on the shelf above the bed.

The brain has its ways of protecting against emotional overload, and the photographer's brain jammed all of a sudden; it refused to budge. The photographer stood in front of the shelf, not moving, her eyes fixed, busy thinking of nothing. Before her, two images were trying to connect: the one that her brain had recorded without her knowing and the one that her eyes were showing her now. The two images were identical, but not yet completely in focus, and once they were, once the two images were perfectly superimposed, one melting into the other, she discovered alongside the absence of the tinplate box the absence of another box, the cardboard box in which Charlie kept his papers, the real ones and the fake ones.

It was only later, paddling on the lake, that the questions, the answers and the anxiety over what was awaiting her came.

Because she got back to work. Sawing, assembling, nailing. She still had another hour before the raft would be satisfactorily assembled, when something inside her told her to go check whether the tinplate box was in Tom's cabin.

It wasn't there.

She had to check one more thing, at Ted's cabin this time. Amid the paint cans scattered about during the police search, she found the box intact and unopened; once she was out on the lake and her brain activity resumed, it confirmed the most dreadful hypothesis. Tom and Charlie had to have brought their boxes of strychnine with them; after all, the police hadn't been interested in Ted's, so why would they have been interested in the other two? She paddled with rage. Could she ever forgive them?

The crossing was made in anger and desperation. She was in a rage, which didn't help her progress. What she needed was more calculation, more rational paddling – a raft is not as easy to manoeuvre as a canoe. It goes every which way if you aren't paying attention to its direction with each stroke of the paddle, and aside from the fact that the photographer had only a crude plank, her thoughts were too consuming for her to manoeuvre so temperamental a watercraft. The point of land she was rowing toward remained remote in spite of all the energy she was putting into it.

She was overwrought, carried by a furious momentum that wasn't subsiding. She was angry with them for having brought Marie-Desneige with them. They had no choice, she realized; she could still understand well enough to see that they couldn't have left Marie-Desneige alone at the hideaway, but did Marie-Desneige have a choice if they decided to short-circuit their brains with strychnine?

The admiration she had had for their pride in their morgue of woodland beasts, their way of defying death, their haughtiness, like a great overlord who decides which is more desirable, life or death – all of what she had admired, envied and even wanted for herself, it was all tarnished in her eyes by the image of Marie-Desneige dying in horrible convulsions.

'They had no right,' she cried out to the vastness of the lake. Her cry came back as an echo. She was halfway there, the point of land still waiting for her, wreathed in the pink sun that was turning the horizon crimson, and behind the postcard landscape, her friends' bay.

'They had no right,' she said, for her own benefit this time. Her inner voice joined with that of Marie-Desneige, nearby, quavering, who had told her, 'I always knew I would have a life.'

The photographer paddled even more furiously. She was kneeling on Marie-Desneige's parka in the centre of the raft. She had brought the parka thinking of the cold nights at the summer camp. She would also have brought Monseigneur for Marie-Desneige to cuddle in the evenings, but she hadn't found the cat, and she paddled and paddled and paddled. Off in the distance, behind the point of land, was a tiny person who had just come to life; she had very few years ahead of her, and her life was being threatened by a tinplate box.

Her back hurt. The pain ran from her shoulders to her shoulder blades and her lower back, at the curve of her spine – it was intolerable, a sharp burning sensation that spread to her buttocks, but she didn't consider changing position or letting up the pace.

Night was falling, its purples and golds scattered in the sky, when a woman absolutely unaware of how exhausted she was landed on the shores of the bay.

She arrived worn out, emptied, her muscles still aching from the effort, legs stiff under her weight and her heart beating like a young girl on a first date. And what if they were waiting for her at the summer camp? What if they were just playing cards and revelling in having escaped the law once again? You can't keep the heart from hoping, and she started down the path that led to the camp with this wild hope, not without noticing the absence of the canoe along the way. *They would have stashed it somewhere else along the shore*, she thought, unworried.

The camp was empty, emptier than it ever had been. The food stores had run dry. Aside from some tinned peaches, there wasn't a single can left on the kitchen shelves. The camp had been lived in. For quite a while, the photographer's glance judged, long enough to deplete the stores of food and make basic necessities disappear, such as candles, pots and, on closer inspection, furs, an axe that was kept inside to make kindling, and, surprisingly enough, a deck of cards. But no damage, no broken windows or door torn from its hinges. Everything was in perfect order. No bears had visited; it had definitely been occupied by humans. Marie-Desneige, Tom and Charlie had stayed here and had left no trace of their stay, aside from the emptiness that only she could recognize and study, out of her mind with worry.

She went back outside and set about searching for what was waiting for her and what she hoped she would not find. The daylight tinged with dusky grey gave less depth but more contrast to the trees and their foliage, the clumps of grass and the slightest rocky protuberance in the ground. The photographer could see very well in it. The lines of shadow gave things more presence, nature laid out before her with more substance; everything was better defined in the sleepy light of the end of the day.

The graves awaited her behind the camp. Two rectangles of earth at the foot of a tall larch, very little space between them and, naturally, no cross, no inscription, nothing to indicate that these were resting places. Two graves side by side: it could only be Marie-Desneige and Charlie. Tom had buried their bodies to protect them from animals, as he had done for Ted, and next spring, nothing would show. Vegetation would take over the rectangles of earth. One dies in the forest as one lives: discreetly, carefully, trying to make no more noise than a leaf in a tree. The photographer could have waxed philosophical – death normally lends itself to that sort of thing – just as she could have asked herself where Tom was, but the combined exhaustion, rage and pain caused her to collapse between the two mounds of earth, and she remained that way for a long time.

She had not fainted. A woman of her build is not so easily incapacitated. Her legs had suddenly refused to carry her, and she found herself nose to the ground between the two graves – strangely, she felt comforted being so close to her friend. Here lies a little old lady, the mound of earth said.

Here lie her hopes and dreams, her life contained in just one year. The rest is of no importance, she did not take it with her, but at her side is her companion, her lover. He loved her like one would love a bird, a rare bird that had come from a long way to nest in the hollow of his hand.

Charlie would continue to watch over Marie-Desneige, the photographer thought.

The anger had dissipated. There was room for nothing but the comfort of knowing they were together. She refused to torture herself with the moments that had accompanied their decision, the words they had exchanged, the last look before the pinch of strychnine. What followed – their death, their burial – she pushed it away with every ounce of strength in her mind. She wanted only to think of their final companionship, their two bodies resting side by side under the layer of earth that protected them and the dusk light that bathed their graves.

But her thoughts turned to Tom. Where had he gone to die? The dead don't bury themselves. He had to have found a place where his body would be protected from animals.

The lake, she told herself, remembering the missing canoe. The lake was the only place he could die in decency.

This thought brought her to her feet and forced her to go check whether the canoe was somewhere else along the shore.

The light was laden with a nighttime grey that was thickening around the outline of the trees and revealed only shapes, furtive movements of silhouettes, shadows amid the shadows. A hare brushed up against her as it ran by.

She walked along the shore up to the big piece of granite and retraced her steps, scanning the black waters of the lake in case she could spot the canoe drifting.

She was sad, sadder thinking of Tom than of Marie-Desneige and Charlie. They had died together, whereas Tom was alone throughout. Had the thought of someone kept him company in his final moments? Tom's life, in spite of all the stories he told, remained a mystery.

She stayed in front of the lake and kept him company until night fell completely and she could see nothing more. She returned to the camp blindly, feeling her way through the darkness and the heaviness of her thoughts.

The night was cold. Her whole body shivered.

She stretched out on the bed, pulled Marie-Desneige's parka over her, hoping to find some warmth and comfort in what was left of her friend. But sleep came only in waves. Too many images jumbled together, too many emotions. She dreamed, half awake, of dogs tearing each other to pieces and wolves howling at the moon. *I forgot about the dogs,* she thought sluggishly. *Where did they bury the dogs?* And she plunged into a wave that carried her off completely.

They are in front of the graves.

Tom is slightly drunk. He has kept his equilibrium, one foot firmly planted and the other ready to take flight, intoxication he consciously delights in the whole time it takes to dig the graves, and now he has just one desire, a glass, and another glass. He wants to die drunk.

It's his final wish.

Charlie accepts, he understands. His old friend wants to go back home. He wants to die where he lived. Marie-Desneige doesn't understand, but she knows that you have to respect a man's dying wishes.

And while Tom sinks further and further into his own private world, Marie-Desneige and Charlie prepare what will be his resting place. They line the bottom of the grave with thick bear skin. It will make for a comfortable bed, Marie-Desneige thinks. It won't make a difference to him, Charlie thinks. He won't have time to feel anything.

Tom is seated, his legs hanging over the grave, his dog beside him. One eye on the bear skin and the other roaming. He is waiting for the moment when he will see his life flash before his eyes. What will he see first? A woman? What woman would be willing to die with him? In every dream where he saw himself dead, there was a woman stretched out alongside him, white and flowery, slowly disappearing into his side.

He presses his dog against him and slides into the grave.

He is not drunk. Well, not as drunk as he had hoped to be. He is completely aware of what is happening. He sees Charlie and Marie-Desneige in a halo of light above him. They are tall, looming and alive. They are immense, and they have promised to stay with him until the end.

'This is where I'm going to spend the winter, Charlie my boy. It's not all that big, but it'll do.'

He is standing in the grave, glass in hand, empty bottle in the other. All three of them know what the empty bottle means. Drink, stretched out on the bearskin, is the only one who doesn't know.

Tom downs his last glass and goes to lie down next to his dog.

Charlie follows each of his friend's gestures. He is worried. He wants it to go well, the strychnine to do its work properly, that there be no blood or vomiting.

'Tom,' he tells him, with a voice that is too slow, too intent, a voice not his own, 'Tom, don't forget, just a pinch, twice that for Drink, otherwise...'

'Otherwise it won't be pretty to watch, eh? Don't worry, I've always known how to conduct myself, particularly when there are women around.'

With that, he takes the box out of his pocket and approaches his dog. With an almost tender gesture, he opens the dog's mouth and drops in a little white rain. Before administering his own fatal dose, he wants to take a final bow, a tip of the hat.

'Go on, a long life to the both of you, and my best wishes to the world.'

And he swallows his pinch.

The effect is not long in coming. Spasmodic movements, convulsions, his arms and legs stiffen, they get intertwined with the dog's legs which scratch him, strike him, lacerate him – the clash of bodies is a horrible thing to see. Charlie had warned him, you're going to get torn apart, but Tom wouldn't bend. 'I want to be with Drink,' and Charlie let him have his way. You couldn't oppose Tom's will. But in that moment, he wants to get down into the grave, remove Drink and let his friend die in peace. It's already too late. The foam has started to form. The end is coming, and Charlie holds Marie-Desneige close to him. Marie-Desneige, who has not said a word, who watches, hypnotized, as death does her work.

The movements that come afterward are heavy and slow. They bury the bodies, Charlie with a shovel and Marie-Desneige with small fistfuls that she lets trickle into the grave. They know that next it will be Darling's turn, Steve's dog, and then Kino, Ted's dog. This is what they had decided the night before. Tom in one grave with Drink and the two other dogs in another. Everything had been said the night before. The goodbyes, words to seal a life, the final handshake, all that had happened the night before at the summer camp. 'I don't want to see another winter,' Tom had said. 'I've lived long enough. This is where it ends for me.'

The dogs' death and burial go as planned. Now they move on to the next step of what awaits them, which is highly uncertain.

They go to the camp and gather what they need. Pots, furs, an axe, a fishing rod, tins. It's Marie-Desneige who thinks to leave a can of peaches on the shelves. 'For Ange-Aimée,' she says. 'Should we leave her a message?'

'Better not,' says Charlie.

They pile their effects in the canoe. Marie-Desneige takes her place in the front, her cat curled up against her. Chummy has found a place to stretch out amidst the jumble in the middle of the canoe. Charlie is in the back. The canoe is weighed down, but he manages in a few pushes of the paddle to extricate the keel from the hold of the sandy bottom, and they are off.

On the shore, a distant presence watches them set off. Death knows she can bide her time. Those two can hope all they like.

AND THE BIRDS RAINED DOWN

In spite of it all, she managed to find a home for the exhibition. Just when she thought she had exhausted all hope, having gone to the last gallery on her list, a young woman who saw the gallery owner turn her down offered her a space that was not a gallery or even an artists' centre, nothing at all quite yet, said the young woman, but a valiant beginning.

The young woman was herself an artist, a glass blower named Clara Wilson, and the place looked like anything but an art gallery. It had been a cooperage for what had been the British Empire's largest distillery. The place was heavy with industrial architecture from another century but was full of possibility, explained Clara, pointing to the rods that would be installed on the ceiling, the steel beams that would be exposed, and the deeply recessed windows in the brick walls, absolutely untouchable, she insisted, for their Victorian beauty. Work would be limited to the essential. Clara was part of a group of cultural activists, and they had limited resources. But everything would be ready in the spring, May at the latest, which suited the photographer, who had a great deal to do in the meantime.

She had not returned to the hideaway. What she had seen had convinced her. Not to say that at times she didn't want to erase the memory of the graves and imagine her friends somewhere, deep in the forest, in a new cabin making another life. But then an image would come to her and wipe out all hope that they were alive: the image of Charlie's shelves with the glaring absence of the tinplate box. And more merciless than the absence of the box of strychnine was the absence of the cardboard box.

That box was precious. It contained Charlie's identification papers, the real ones and the fake ones, and cash, lots of cash. Charlie had shown her the contents just before she left for Toronto. For Marie-Desneige, he had told her, if ever she is no longer happy in the forest. The photographer had been impressed by the number of bills it contained. Denominations of one hundred dollars held in large elastics. Several rolls, thousands of dollars, the photographer guessed. She couldn't help but whistle in surprise. *My government cheques,* Charlie had explained. *I never managed to spend it all.*

For Marie-Desneige, he stressed again.

And she had promised. She would find somewhere for her. She would take care of her, if one day Marie-Desneige no longer wanted to live at the hideaway.

She understood from the great relief in Charlie's eyes that he was prepared to sacrifice anything for Marie-Desneige's happiness. Their attentiveness to one another, that tenderness in their eyes, all of what she had taken as a pleasant little amorous friendship, one last affair of the heart, was a much deeper feeling. They loved each other as people love each other at the age of twenty. The absence of the two boxes on Charlie's shelves could mean only one thing: they had decided to perish together, absolutely and definitively, leaving no trace.

She ended up accepting the unacceptable. How can you stand in the way of love? Over the months, the two missing boxes became a supremely romantic image. Charlie and Marie-Desneige walking hand in hand, Romeo and Juliet heading off to meet their destiny.

Steve and Bruno, however, were alive. Steve was in jail in Monteith, with no hope of bail, the judge having decided that that there was too much evidence that this man would return to the woods the first chance he got. As for Bruno, there had been no news. He wasn't there when the police raided and had not shown his face in the area since. Neither was it in the photographer's interest to hang about the place, because they were looking for accomplices.

That's what she had been given to understand by Jerry, the hotel owner who served as a mail drop for the government cheques that Steve went to cash at the end of the month.

'And the others?' she had asked without naming them.

'The others?' he said, raising an eyebrow.

It was clear that he had never believed that Tom and Charlie existed, even less so the reclusive old woman deep in the woods. He believed only in petty trafficking, in what he could skim here and there from other people's schemes.

She had not gone back to the short, potbellied man's hotel.

The months that followed were filled with preparing for the exhibition. It was all she had left of the year spent with her old friends in the woods. Three-hundred and sixty-six paintings, Ted's haunted pain and Marie-Desneige's gaze, which had shed light on every splash of colour. The paintings for the exhibition were cluttering up her apartment. The others were in a warehouse in the north of the city.

Sometimes she would wake up at night, roused by a nightmare that she couldn't remember any scenes from, and would walk through the rooms of the apartment to find a burst of colour in the paintings that would take her back to the deep woods and her friends.

Work was her salvation. Aside from the exhibition, different commissions occupied her almost to the point of exhaustion. She had plenty to think about, to do and to decide.

Fortunately, there was Clara. The young woman was a whiff of spring, her friends just as sunny, and she let herself be caught up in their energy. They were thrilled with the idea of presenting the work of an unknown artist, an original, an independent who had had no teacher, a raw talent, a force of inspiration, a grand master of composition. There was no shortage of praise. They admired her photos as well. She was very pleased with her bellowed Wista for producing this textured light and the depth of gaze.

The project took off like a shot. At times it made her dizzy. They wanted to pull out all the stops for this exhibition. They had not made whiskey in the old distillery for years, but the immensity of the place, the old stone and the old-fashioned cobblestone roads, fuelled rumours of all sorts, the most reliable of which was that it was being turned into something bohemian chic, with restaurants, theatres, galleries and boutiques, a bit in the image of Yorkville of days past, but more European. Clara and her friends wanted to be front and centre when the arts, the evening strollers and fine dining took the place over.

For the time being, the old distillery served as a shooting location. A Hollywood crew shooting a period farce had been charmed by the young people and had left them part of the cooperage.

The photographer had carte blanche. They liked the concept of the exhibition. Paintings and photos that spoke to one another, and particularly this whole new story, the Great Matheson Fire, a half-blind boy wandering through the rubble looking not for one lover but for two, absolutely identical, who would hold him the rest of his life in the tangled threads of a love that could not be. Love, wandering, pain, the deep woods and redemption through art – all themes dear to the hearts of young artists who love it when life scrapes the depths before ascending to the light.

At the centre of their interest was the series *Young Girls with Long Hair*, from which they had decided to keep only five pieces. The arrival from the distance of a raft on the river, streaks of gold in the black waters. The raft, seen from closer up, and two young girls with golden hair paddling with their hands. Seen from closer still, the young girls see someone on the shore, signalling to them, beseeching them. The drama of the next scene when the raft capsizes in an eddy of black water. And the final close-up on the strange beauty of their faces.

The series should have been accompanied by the photo of Angie Polson, the only survivor of this romantic tragedy. But the photographer's failure to act, that missed click in High Park when she had the old woman before her, deprived the series of the only possible photo of Angie Polson.

In its stead, there was the portrait Ted Boychuck had painted of her. In this portrait, Angie Polson was younger than the little old lady of High Park, twenty or thirty years younger, but with the same twinkling pink light in the corner of her eyes.

Under the portrait, a caption card.

> Angie Polson, between 1965 and 1975. Born in Matheson in 1902. With her twin sister, Margie, she survived the Great Fire by escaping along the Black River on a makeshift raft. In 1920, she left Matheson for Toronto. The rest of her life is a mystery. She was last seen in Matheson in 1972 and in High Park in Toronto in the spring of 1994. Her twin sister died of cancer in 1969.

Clara didn't like it. Too cold, too official, the text disavowed any emotion; it hid the beauty, the love, the passion, and *The rest of her life is a mystery* was untrue, patently untrue. We know that her life was consumed by a failed love triangle involving her sister. And that this love was hopeless because they loved a man who was incapable of love. And that this man is dead, leaving behind him an oeuvre that pays tribute to their beauty. So why be evasive, elusive, dodge the question?

The photographer removed her caption and drafted this:

> Angie Polson, between 1965 and 1975. Born in Matheson in 1902. With her twin sister, Margie, she survived the Great Fire by escaping along the Black River on a makeshift raft. The young Boychuck wandered for days searching for them, and, not finding them, left Matheson. He returned in 1922, at which point Margie was married and Angie was waiting for him in Toronto. What followed was a long series of more or less failed rendezvous. Their entire lives, they would be bound by an impossible love. Margie died in 1969, Ted Boychuck in 1996. Only Angie is still alive. She was seen in the spring of 1994 in High Park, Toronto.

She was fairly satisfied with the ending, which left the mystery hanging. She would have liked to have added *She was feeding the birds,* but she was limited by the number of lines the card could hold. In any case, she told herself, the question was implicit. And what about you? Have you seen her in High Park or anywhere else?

She wanted to find the little old bird lady. She was unaware of her own intention until the word *bird* came back into her head, ready to be written down on the too-small card. She knew then that this exhibition had no other goal than to flush out the little old lady, wherever she may be.

'It was raining birds,' the little old lady had said.

'It was raining birds?' Clara asked.

The photographer had just found the title for the exhibition.

A title that, if it fell under the eyes of the person in question, couldn't help but bring her back to her.

On the first nice day of April, the photographer went to High Park, with one foot in spring and the other she didn't know where. She dreamed of fir bushes, vast lakes, pure air that fills the chest, and a little old lady waiting on the bench.

Angie Polson wasn't there. Wishing it wasn't enough to make it so. In her stead, there was a man. Firmly propped up on the bench, his legs stretched out in front of him, his hands in the pockets of his overcoat, the man was lost in thought. *In his early fifties*, the photographer thought. *Nice build*, she thought some more. The man was imposing, in fact. Seated comfortably at the end of the bench, he gave the impression of filling it entirely. And his hair, which was a nice dark grey, formed a downy foam all around his head. She thought of Marie-Desneige.

A flock of low-flying pigeons came to rest at the man's feet. Her thoughts turned to Angie Polson and her square of cotton.

The man became aware of the photographer's presence, offered an embarrassed smile, *sorry*, the smile said, *I took your place*, and with a gesture of the hand, invited her to sit near him.

He wanted to be far away, very far away, to no longer have to deal with anything, to lose himself at the ends of the earth, to no longer have to explain himself to anyone. He was tired of it all. Of work, of responsibilities, of all that was expected of him. That's what he explained to the photographer in a weary voice as she fed the pigeons with the piece of bread she had brought. 'I would like to disappear,' he said again, 'to become invisible. I want to exist for no one.'

'I know a place, but you're too young.'

The photographer listened to the weary voice, but her attention was elsewhere. In the man's nice build she could picture a place for herself, a warm, comfortable place, a man's enveloping heat where she could see herself welcomed with two arms folded around her.

His name was Richard Bernatchez. That's what he told her. *Richard the Lionhearted,* she thought to herself without knowing why. The heart of a valiant king.

And when, in turn, he asked for her name, she gave it to him in full, thinking of her friends in the woods, whom she had known under false names and whom she would never seen again.

'That's a nice name,' Richard the Lionhearted told her.

A small house under the trees on the road out of a village. From the road, you can see the cedar shingle facade and the gable that reaches out to offer the veranda some shade. The curtains are drawn, probably to keep a bit of coolness inside the house. It is a hot summer's day. An old man is getting some fresh air on the veranda.

Charlie smokes a cigarette while nibbling at a sprig of millet.

'So, are you coming?'

He is a little thinner, with two long grooves in his cheeks, but as for the rest of him, he still has all the vigour of his ninety-one years. He made the return trip to the village under the sun, and now he is getting some fresh air. A nice cigarette, a cold glass of water, life still has its pleasures.

'It's time,' he calls out in the direction of the screen door.

'I'm coming, I'm coming.'

Marie-Desneige's frothy head appears in the half-open door. White and luminous. She creeps cautiously with a tea tray and Monseigneur winding around her legs.

She is wearing a pale dress. Blue and coral pink that give her hair even more sheen.

She lays the tray on a sideboard near the double rocker and sits down next to Charlie. He has been waiting for her for a while, because he has a small victory in his hands. Two envelopes he has not opened. They both know what they contain. Their pension cheques. Charlie was confident, but Marie-Desneige didn't believe it. She didn't believe that the government cheques could follow them here, here to this village where no one knew them. But Charlie had been a postman. He knew how to do it.

'There was nothing else?'

Each time he returns from the post office, it's the same question.

'No, nothing else.'

'We should write to her.'

'How do you want to do that? We don't have her address, or even her name.'

Marie-Desneige sighs. They often have this discussion. Marie-Desneige, who wants to see her friend again, and Charlie, who explains that it is better this way. It's time for the woman to live her own life.

Chummy, who is at the other end of the veranda, gets up and comes to stretch out next to Charlie. He knows that it's time. The two old people rocking gently in the rocking chair, Monseigneur in the arms of Marie-Desneige, and Chummy who consents to Charlie scratching him.

The villagers will be coming back from their jobs in town. The parade of cars will be starting soon.

The story does not reveal the location of the village or its name. Silence is better than needless words, particularly when it comes to happiness, and when that happiness is fragile.

Happiness needs only your consent. Marie-Desneige and Charlie have a few years left in them, and they intend to make those years into a lifetime. They will stay hidden away from the eyes of the world.

There are a number of loose ends in this story. Like the letter that arrived at the cooperage well after the exhibition had been dismantled and the film crew had returned to Hollywood. A letter signed Angie Polson. The old woman had visited the exhibition and wanted to clarify the date Theodore had painted her portrait.

It is not known whether the letter reached its intended recipient.

The exhibition had been a success. All the paintings sold, and there was an article full of praise in the Globe and Mail. *The money from the sale of the paintings was placed in trust and awaits a turn in the story.*

And death? Well, she is still prowling. But pay her no mind. She lurks in every story.

ACKNOWLEDGMENTS

Tremendous thanks from the author:

To Sylvia and Mike Milinkovich, who introduced me to William Hough, Robert Rhodes and the marvellous Jessie Dambrowitch, eighty-nine years old, who recalled for me that his father had seen birds falling from the sky.

To the team at XYZ and above all to André Vanasse, who has watched over my novels from the first.

Thanks from the translator to Jocelyne Saucier for her generosity, Alana Wilcox and Coach House Books for doing such a fine job, the query lunchers for their insight and company, and Fabrice Laurent for the French lessons.

Jocelyne Saucier was born in New Brunswick. Two of her previous novels, *La vie comme une imae* and *Jeanne sur les routes*, were finalists for the Governor General's Award. *Il pleuvait des oiseaux* garnered her the Prix des Cinq Continents de la Francophonie, making her the first Canadian to win the award. She lives in Abitibi, Québec.

Rhonda Mullins is a translator, writer and editor. She was a finalist for the 2007 Governor General's Literary Award for Translation for *The Decline of the Hollywood Empire* by Hervé Fischer. She previously translated Jocelyne Saucier's *Jeanne sur les routes* into *Jeanne's Road* (2010, Cormorant Books). She lives in Montreal.

Typeset in Ronaldson, the very first American metal typeface, which was designed by Alexander Kay in 1884, for the Mackeller, Smiths, & Jordan type foundry of Philadelphia, and was lost to time until it was digitized in 2006 by Patrick Griffin of Canada Type.

Printed at the old Coach House on bpNichol Lane in Toronto, Ontario, on Zephyr Antique Laid paper, which was manufactured, acid-free, in Saint-Jérôme, Quebec, from second-growth forests. This book was printed with vegetable-based ink on a 1965 Heidelberg KORD offset litho press. Its pages were folded on a Baumfolder, gathered by hand, bound on a Sulby Auto-Minabinda and trimmed on a Polar single-knife cutter.

Edited and designed by Alana Wilcox
Photo of Jocelyne Saucier by Cyclopes
Photo of Rhonda Mullins by Owen Egan

Coach House Books
80 bpNichol Lane
Toronto ON M5S 3J4
Canada

416 979 2217
800 367 6360

mail@chbooks.com
www.chbooks.com